FULL MOON

ff

FULL MOON

Kenneth
Lillington

faber and faber

LONDON · BOSTON

First published in 1986
by Faber and Faber Limited
3 Queen Square London WC1N 3AU

Printed in Great Britain by
Butler & Tanner Ltd., Frome, Somerset

British Library Cataloguing in Publication Data
Lillington, Kenneth
Full moon.
I. Title
823'.914[J]   PZ7
ISBN 0-571-13792-X

For Rosalind Choat

CHAPTER ONE

When we were little, seven or so, my sister Jennifer used to tell me that our great-aunt's shop was haunted. She said that the dolls on the upper floors came to life at night and would link hands across the landing and hold you at bay. You had to go along that landing for the lavatory, and when we visited the shop I would suffer agonies rather than risk it.

Jennifer said that when there was a full moon our great-aunt would fly over the housetops on a birch-broom. This made me giggle at mealtimes, and my father would order me from the table in a rage, but at night I would cower under the bedclothes, and I was always asking my exasperated mother when it would be full moon.

One winter evening, when we were visiting, Jennifer gave me a smuggy little-girl glance and went off to that dreaded landing herself. Something – fearful curiosity, or a vague will to protect her, I don't know what – made me slip out after her. Being too much of a coward to mount guard at the top of the stairs, I found a light switch and threw it. This, as it happened, lit up the glass cases where the dolls were displayed. There was a shriek from the floor above. I yelled, 'The dolls, the dolls!', certain that they had come to life, and my father dashed upstairs and carried Jennifer down. She sobbed and sobbed: 'It's *his* fault! It's all *his* fault!' I wailed: 'I didn't do anything! *She* told me . . .' My great-aunt was a statue of icy disdain; my mother stammered apologies; and my father consoled Jennifer, with his back to me, as if he were hiding her from me.

He worshipped Jennifer. And as the years went by it got worse. He was a teacher in a sixth form college. He expected her to become a university lecturer, which for him was as far as anyone could go. He coached her and loaded her with books. She had already got a clutch of O Levels like a royal flush, and she was halfway to doing the same with A Levels. Once, when I was about eleven, I heard him say, 'Of course, you couldn't expect two in one family like Jennifer. We should be thankful we've got one of her . . . Yes, they are widely apart in ability, I'm afraid . . .'

Yes. If ability were a dress, I should have walked behind Jennifer, holding her train.

Over the years our great-aunt became eccentric to the point of lunacy. She would stand, late at night, behind the glass door at the front of the shop, tall and gaunt in a white nightdress like a winding-sheet. Passers-by could mistake her for a model. Then she would suddenly thrust out a bony forefinger and, apparently, gibber curses. It must have been unnerving for people ambling home from the village pub.

My father worried about her. He said that she was no longer capable of running a shop full of valuable antiques. My father studied them, of course, in books: *Miller's Guide, Glass, Silver, Clocks and Watches,* etc etc. My mother kept going to the antiques fairs and the shops.

I once heard my father say, quietly, 'You wouldn't give up your job?'

'Oh no, not at first.' (Mother was a teacher in a junior school.)

'It isn't far to travel, and we could get someone in to help out.'

'That would be best.'

'Always assuming, of course . . . !'

'Quite!'

Our great-aunt resisted all offers of help. Whenever we

8

entered the shop she would huddle over whatever object was nearest to her, glowering like an animal over its food. But, for all my father's anxiety, she was never swindled. She remained a good business woman to her dying day.

Her dying day was a bitterly cold one in mid-January. We were glad of the warmth in the crematorium chapel. Of the four of us, my father looked the most upset, as seemed proper in the only nephew of a wealthy spinster. He knitted his brows and sadly shook his head, as if unable to come to terms with his sorrow. Part of this was acting, but quite a lot of it was because he was worrying about his car. It had taken a long time to start that morning. He always worried terribly whenever it went wrong.

We were the only mourners, except for one young girl, standing aloof on the other side of the chapel. We were not in black, just soberly dressed, but she had made an attempt at mourning with a black jacket over a grey skirt, and a black ribbon tie on a white blouse. She kept looking at us, but whenever I caught her eye she looked away to the parson, quickly, and as soon as the service was ended she hurried away before we could speak to her.

'Who was she?' whispered Jennifer, as we drifted away.

'Never seen her before,' said my father.

'She kept staring at us.'

'Yes, I didn't think she liked us very much.'

Another furrow appeared in my father's brow. Perhaps the girl was a rival claimant, out of the blue.

He need not have worried. Our great-aunt left the shop, contents and all, to him: 'To my only living relative, Andrew, for want of someone better.'

'She need not have added that.'

'We mustn't look a gift-horse in the mouth,' said my mother cheerfully.

It was a gift all right. We could sell our own semi-detached and move in. Imagine being able to sell a house without having to buy another one! The shop was rather run down, but in a good position at the quiet end of the high street, among the cafés and the other antiques shops, and it could attract good custom. A lot of tourists visited the Cotswolds in the summer.

All that spring we put up with house-hunters prowling round our home, saying how lovely it was, and disappearing without another word, but at last we sold it, and just before Easter we moved into the shop.

As the removal men clumped through it, I picked my way through the dust-sheeted junk and went down to the basement, which had been out of bounds while our great-aunt was alive. The bric-à-brac was stowed away down here: bundles of old magazines and papers, flyblown prints, a microscope, some handbells, a marble-topped washstand, a mangle, and an ancient telephone, labelled 'c.1888', in black and gilt, with two rusty bells on its stand. I picked this up, and found it had a foot and a half of rotted and raw-ended flex dangling from it.

There were three light-fittings, but only one had a bulb in it, and that blew when I threw the switch. I found the fuse-box and mended the fuse with a safety-pin from a pincushion sewn over with beads. The fuse-box was in a narrow cupboard in a corner. I shone my torch in, and discovered something that sent my memory back ten years. I went back upstairs.

'Jen! Come here!'

'Remember the witch's broom?' I said. 'I've found it.'

She hung back at the foot of the stairs.

'Can't we have a light on?'

'No, I'll have to get a new bulb and check the wiring.'

'This place is like a morgue.'

'Look, here it is.'

From the cupboard I fished an old birch-broom, dusty and black with age.

'Care for a trial spin?'

She took hold of the handle, gingerly.

'That old witch,' she said. 'She probably *did*, you know–'

Then she thrust the broom away from her.

'Put it back in the cupboard!'

'All right!'

'Well, go on then. Shut the cupboard, and let's get out of here.'

'What's up?' I said, as we reached the top of the stairs.

'That's a horrible place. I'm not going down there again.'

My intellectual sister had one weakness: she was afraid of the dark. You remember what it was like when you were a child, being scared and staying scared even after you knew the cause? The dressing-gown on the bedroom door that still looked like a hanged man, the patch on the ceiling that remained a wicked, sagging face? Jennifer had never got over this.

My father made a virtue of it. 'One has to pay for being ultra-sensitive,' he said. In our old house, he had had a dimmer-switch fixed in her bedroom.

For as long as I could remember, there had been a current between my twin sister and me. 'Current' is not a good word for it, but it's the best I can find. It was not exactly thought-reading; 'feelings-reading' would be more like it: a sense of each other's mood. It had nothing to do with love or liking. You are close to your left ear without necessarily loving it. But I think that if one of us had ever been missing, the other could have gone to the spot, like a tracker dog.

People would say how close we were, and it always put my father out of temper when they did.

I knew that she was nervous in this new house, and I was not surprised when she tapped at my door that night.

'You awake? . . . Come in a minute, will you?'

My father was awake too. There was no current between him and Jennifer, but I think he must have had some private

11

circuit to her, like a burglar alarm. No sooner were we in her room than he came on to the landing.

'Anything wrong, Jenny?'

Jennifer raised her eyes to heaven. 'It's all right, Dad. My – my lamp's not working and I'm just getting John to look at it.'

'It seems to be on all right.'

'Sometimes it flickers.'

'Well,' said my father begrudgingly, 'see to it then, John.' I was the family handyman, as befitted my lowly academic status. 'She must get some sleep.'

I thought he might stay to watch, but he never liked seeing me take charge of Jennifer's needs.

'It's the dolls,' whispered Jennifer, when he had gone. 'I don't like the way they look at me.'

We never needed to explain our feelings. 'I can't move them tonight, Jen.'

'Tomorrow, then?'

'All right.'

'Stay and talk to me.'

'Be your age. Come on, you know quite well you're nuts. Celluloid and hair, they are. They can't look at you through the wall.'

She eyed me in silence.

'There's a screen in the landing cupboard,' I said. 'I'll fix it in front of them.'

'Do that, then.'

The next day I asked my father if I could move the dolls to another place. I hoped for some look in the eye to show that he understood my reasons, but all I got was a curt 'If you like'. The dolls were in glass cases on either side of the landing. A swing-gate marked 'Private' cut them off from the living quarters. They looked at you as you came through their ranks, and they looked at you on the way back, because they were arranged each way, some facing, some turning their backs.

This really was quite spooky; it made them seem to follow you round with their eyes. But once out of their cases, they were nothing, just china or modelling stuff, some sophisticated, some blue-eyed and chubby-cheeked; and they went on smiling whatever you did to them.

As Jennifer had said she would never go down to the basement I took them there, and arranged them on two shelves where the light fell on them. I tried to keep them in the order they had been in in the cases upstairs, putting the left-hand lot on the lower shelf, and the right on the higher. I stood back and surveyed them: the Edwardian ones with their lace collars, the Spanish ones you could imagine twirling their skirts and rattling castanets.

I said aloud, 'Sorry about this, but my sister suspects you of witchcraft.'

They hissed at me.

I was sure they did. I jumped back about three feet. They stared back at me with their silly fixed faces. But I had heard them hiss, spitefully, like cats. I am afraid I panicked. I bolted to the top of the stairs, knocking over a chair. Then I pulled myself together. This was ridiculous. Jennifer had frightened herself and me when we were kids, and these twitching brooms and hissing dolls must be some psychological thing, the unconscious mind hiccupping.

Actually I find psychological explanations harder to believe in than ghosts. Nevertheless I went down again and forced myself to pick one of them up. Its lips were a tiny, bright red Cupid's bow, just showing a line of miniature teeth. To hiss you must draw out the corners of your mouth. It couldn't possibly do that. I had fooled myself; or else a ventriloquist was at work.

I said nothing to Jennifer, but to keep telling myself that it was all nonsense meant that I was always thinking about it, and she was too much on my wavelength not to sense that. You'd think

13

she could have asked me about it, but this was something we could never do. 'The current' never ran into words. All that day she was moody, apparently lost in thought. My father kept an apprehensive eye on her.

'Not worrying about A Levels, Jenny? You'll cake-walk them.'

'Dad, I am *not* worrying about A Levels.'

'Well, you could have fooled me. Anything else, then?'

'No, Dad, *nothing at all.*'

That night I woke to hear voices coming from Jennifer's room. They were female and shrill. I could not make out the words, but the noise, I should think, could have been heard in the dress-shop on the other side of the street. I wondered whatever sort of party she could be throwing, and marvelled at her nerve. I put on my dressing-gown and went out to the landing, and was amazed that my father didn't come out too. Surely such a light sleeper could hear this racket? I waited outside Jennifer's door. I still could not make out what was being said, but the row was louder still. Jennifer's own voice was not to be heard. I thought: antiques shop – burglars! There were some weaknesses in this explanation, but I didn't stop to consider them. I bunched my muscles and threw open her door.

The room was empty, except for Jennifer herself, in her bed. She whimpered a little. She brought up both fists and pressed them to her forehead. She rolled on her side.

As soon as I saw her, the racket stopped; and immediately, I understood. I knelt by her bed.

'Jen–'

She sat up and looked at me blankly. She said 'O-oh!' and held her face in her hands. She took her hands away and woke up.

'I was having a horrible dream. There were these two women. They seemed to be having some sort of hysterical quarrel. I was in between them and trying to stop them and

14

they wouldn't listen–'

'Yes, I know,' I said. 'I heard them too.'

Which was the simple truth. I had heard them quarrelling in my sister's dream. No wonder my father had heard nothing.

'I heard them,' I repeated. 'They've gone. You're all right.'

She showed no surprise. She understood. 'Did you?' she said.

'You're all right. Jen, do you know who they were?'

'No.'

'Could you make out what they were saying?'

'No, that was awful, it was all . . . scrambled. I tried to make sense of it, but it sounded like gibberish. I–I–'

'Yes, all right. You're O.K. now. Tell me in the morning.'

To enter someone else's dream is a gross invasion of privacy, and Jennifer needed to be left alone, but, as I feared, my father heard us, and interfered at this point. I could have killed him.

'Anything wrong, Jenny?'

He came into her bedroom. Jennifer shrieked:

'I don't want you, Dad! Go away! For God's sake *go away!*'

He was bitterly hurt.

'Very well, very well. We'd all better go away and let you calm down. You might think I have a right to ask just what's going on . . .'

And now I felt sorry for him. 'She's upset, Dad. She's been having a nightmare.'

'And how did you know that? Did she call you?'

'No. I just knew.'

He looked at me with bitter dislike. 'Really? So mind-reading is one of your many gifts, is it?'

Stupid bloody schoolteachery pompous sarcasm! All my sympathy evaporated. I clenched my fists. A first-class row hung in the balance, but my mother came into the bedroom, bringing calm with her.

My father became authoritative. 'She's been having a nightmare, that's all. She's run down. This move has

15

disturbed her.'

'I see,' said my mother, in her mild voice. She looked down at my pale and cornered twin and ruffled her hair slightly. She was never demonstrative with Jennifer, and gave the impression of never taking her wholly seriously. 'You're finding life rather difficult just now, aren't you, dear?'

This was typically vague. But oddly enough, full of insight.

CHAPTER TWO

Curiously enough, the next morning we all felt better for it. My father made overtures to Jennifer and Jennifer apologized to my father, which quite made his day. It was as if a storm had passed over, and I even wondered whether some last, lingering spirit had finally left the house.

When we were having elevenses in the back room among the now unveiled antiques, we were visited by the girl we had seen at the funeral. She followed my mother from the front door, but stopped in the doorway.

'I've brought back the key,' she said.

She looked at each of us in turn, uncertain, half timid and half defiant. She was wearing the same grey skirt she had worn at the funeral, with a grey cable-stitched jumper. She had large, sad brown eyes.

'The *key?*' said my father, in the bantering tone he used with girls. 'Well now: who are you?'

'Rosalind.'

'Well now,' said my father, 'that is probably not an inexact or insulting description of yourself, but it doesn't give much away. Could you enlarge a little, please?'

'Sorry?'

'My husband wants to know how you came by the key,' said my mother. 'Coffee, Rosalind?'

'No thank you. Yes, well, the old lady gave me the key. I used to do things for her, cook for her, run errands and that.'

'Home Help?'

'Sort of, but I was acting on my own, not, like, paid or anything.'

'Altruistic,' said my father.

'Sorry?'

'You acted out of kindness,' translated my mother.

'Oh, well, she needed looking after.'

'Well,' said my father uncomfortably, 'it was not for want of trying on our part, I assure you, but she was by no means an easy person.' The girl was watching him with level eyes, and he became slightly nettled. 'You've kept that key a long time.'

'Till you moved in. I didn't like to put it through the letterbox.'

'You could have given it to the agents.'

'Didn't know about them.'

'Biscuit?' said my mother.

'No thank you.'

She nodded briefly and turned to go, like, I thought, a cat that makes a dash for it, but my mother was studying her, amiably.

'Rosalind, if we wanted to get in touch with you, where could we find you?'

'Rainham Foundation.'

The Rainham Foundation was a Children's Home. 'Yes, I know it,' said my mother, with interest. 'One or two children at the school come from it. They look after you well there, don't they?'

'Yes.'

'If I rang, who should I ask for?'

'Rosalind.'

'Just Rosalind?'

'Yes.'

'Well, thank you for calling, Rosalind.'

'That was what I'd call monosyllabic,' said Jennifer, when the girl had gone.

'When I opened the door to her, she stammered something

18

and tried to bolt for it,' said my mother. 'I practically had to drag her in.'

'Weird,' said Jennifer. 'I hate weird people.'

'Oh, couldn't you see she was scared stiff of us? I think she's lonely. I know Claire Waltham at the Rainham. I'll have a word with her.'

'You mind what you're doing,' said my father. 'Don't go making her another of your lame dogs.'

'She seems to have made herself pretty useful, for a lame dog. She must have been patient to look after your aunt for nothing.'

'Yes, a saint,' said my father. 'She looks like one, too, with that grave air of hers. She's probably made of alabaster.'

'Needs sympathy,' said Jennifer. 'I hate people who need sympathy. All the same, those fabulous brown eyes! I wish I looked like that. There you are, John, a nice, problem, girl-friend for you.'

'Alas,' I said, 'she would never look at poor, dowdy me.'

'No, you've hit the nail on the head.'

Rosalind? said Mrs Waltham, of the Rainham Foundation. Yes, excellent. Entirely trustworthy. Marvellous with children and old people, the more difficult the better. Yes, by all reports, she'd handled Miss Crawley (our great-aunt) superbly, neither sloppy nor bossy; treated her as a friend . . . How had she got to know her? Oh, Rosalind had a flair for discovering old people in need of help . . .

Mind, you could never get much out of her . . . yes, extremely reserved. Dodged giving her surname? Ah yes, she hated her surname . . . Rosalind Castle. She'd been found in a church porch in Castle Street in the next town . . . No, parents unknown . . . She was wont to say that they might as well have called her Rosalind Back Alley . . . Oh no, no, not bitter, very affectionate, really . . . Well, she was absolutely set on becoming a nurse, but she was too young as yet . . .

'I think,' said my mother, 'that she's just what we need to help us in the shop.'

'Would she want to?' said my father. 'We're not children and we're not yet geriatric, I hope.'

'I think she'd love to.'

'M'm,' mused my father. 'Parent-substitutes, eh?'

'If you like,' said my mother placidly.

Rosalind accepted my mother's offer, politely, but without the least gush; yet I believe that inside her she was quivering with delight and gratitude. She was doing a part-time pre-nursing course at the Tech., and served in the shop when she was free. This worked quite well, because antiques shops in general keep very irregular hours. Once Jennifer and I had gone back to college after the Easter holidays, we didn't see much of her. She seemed perfectly happy. It dawned on me that she was beautiful. Her face, relaxed in happiness, was dreamily lovely, as if she were lost in long, long thoughts.

'*Une jeune fille supérieure,*' murmured my mother.

'What?'

'Nothing,' said my mother. 'Just mumbling to myself.'

She asked Rosalind no questions. 'She'll tell us in her own good time.'

Everyone began to notice Rosalind's looks, not least the customers. Jennifer, who was generous enough when she wasn't being sarcastic, said 'dishy'. My father said she had classical features. But I am afraid that 'unreachable' was my word for her.

She knew the shop like an expert.

'Well, I had to learn, because Miss Crawley liked to talk about it, see.'

'She ought to have left you something, Rosalind,' said my mother.

'She did. A photograph album.'

'Is that all?' said Jennifer.

'Oh, I could have had anything if I'd wanted it. A few weeks before she died, she said, well, Rosalind, my number's up–she said yes it is, child, don't argue–and I'd like to give you something before the–er–'

'The vultures gather?' suggested Jennifer.

'I'm sure she didn't say that,' said Rosalind uncomfortably. 'Anyway, she said, you can have anything you like from the shop. Go on, she said, you like nice things, don't you? I said, I can get along without that, Miss Crawley, and I really meant it, I didn't want her things. They're only things.'

Then, realizing that she was surrounded by things, our things, she blushed.

'Quite right,' said my mother. 'What did she say to that?'

'Argued, but in the end she said, good, you're right, girl, they're *things,* and they don't bring happiness. But they're my substitute for a life, she said. And she said, I'm going to give you something I treasure very much, and you must treasure it too. And she gave me this family album. And she said, all the people in this album are at peace now, except one, and she soon will be, I hope. And she said, there's a world of heartache in this album, Rosalind. It would be worth a few pounds in the shop, and it's worth all the other things put together.'

'And do you treasure it, Rosalind?'

'Yes,' said Rosalind, and suddenly–possibly for the first time in her life–she smiled. If she smiled like this at her future patients, I thought, she could save them from death. 'Yes, I do. I didn't know what to make of it at first, but I do treasure it, yes. I kid myself that they're my own family.'

It loosened her up, this conversation. One Saturday morning, when I was fixing something in the shop, she said to me abruptly:

'You reckon I'm daft, hating my name?'

'No, but it's a perfectly good name.'

'I hate it.'

'Well,' I said, not certain how to proceed, 'I don't see why you shouldn't if you want to. Some people go mad at certain words, like fascist or communist.'

'Yes, right, they do. Your auntie did. There was one word made her go spare. You know what it was?'

'Sex?'

'No. *Witch*.'

My eyes widened. 'Was it, though?' I said.

'Easy to see why. The people round here began calling her one, and she didn't like it, who would?'

'She asked for it, though, standing at the door at midnight cursing people.'

'She was not cursing them, she was terrified, what with the telly and the papers full of burglars murdering rich old women and muggings and that: she got so uptight she'd have to get out of bed and keep watch. Just ordering them away, she was.'

'You know a lot about her.'

'No, not really. She kept herself very much to herself.'

'How did you meet her, Rosalind?'

It seemed that Rosalind had happened to pass the shop when my great-aunt, an emaciated eighty-three, was trying to lug a heavy bureau into position. She went in and lent a hand. My great-aunt took her for a teenage thug and screeched abuse, but Rosalind took no notice, dragged the bureau round unaided, said, 'There – is that where you want it?' and made to leave. My great-aunt, still eyeing her suspiciously, then gave her a chocolate.

'If you're reorganizing your shop,' said Rosalind, 'you'll need me again, won't you?'

'You won't get any more chocolates.'

'I'll bring you some.' And Rosalind began calling on the old lady regularly.

'And after that she was nice to you, was she?'

'Oh no, awful. The better I got to know her, the more she bawled me out. "Not *there*, you stupid girl! Mind what you're doing! Why are you so clumsy?"'

'And you put up with it?'

22

'Had to, didn't I? Anyway, being nice doesn't mean anything.'

'What's one supposed to be, then?'

'Oh, you know. All my life people have been *nice,* in specially nice voices, because they know what I am. Anyway, she wasn't nice. But one day she went too far. She said, "You clumsy, ill-bred girl, where were you dragged-up?" And I wagged my finger under her nose and I said, "Now listen, if you ever say that again I'm going to walk out and never come back." She was like a naughty child in some ways, and it shook her. "Yes, you're right to be angry. Who am I, to talk about upbringing?" And she was never rude to me again. I practically moved in. I washed and cooked for her, and that. Poor old thing.'

'I think you were very fond of her.'

'I loved her.'

'Well,' I said, after a considerable pause, 'I hope she loved you back.'

'Can't tell, can you?

'I knew her for just over two years. Towards the end she got very strange. She used to talk to herself non-stop. Once I walked in on her, sitting up there on the landing among the dolls, rattling on at the top of her voice. I made a joke of it. I said, "Hallo, having a good natter, then?" She gave me a sort of mad look. Her eyes were all lost and staring. White circles round their pupils. She said in a croaky voice, "Natter. Yes, a good natter, my dear. To my sister below."'

'Below!'

'Yes. Do you know, it gave me goose-flesh, that did.'

'Rosalind, what did she mean, *below?*'

I sat on the edge of a chair, facing her. She was sitting on a table, with her back to the May sunlight which poured over her silky brown hair. Haloed like this, she looked like a madonna. I gazed up at her. At that moment Jennifer came into the shop from the back.

'Oh!' she said significantly. 'Excuse *me,'* and went out again.

'Berk,' I muttered.

'Do you like having a twin sister?'

'Well, not always.'

'You two are terrifically close, aren't you?'

'Why?'

'Anyone can see. Do you know,' added Rosalind irrelevantly, 'you call her Jen when you speak to her, but Jennifer when you speak about her?'

'Oh, do I? Close? We may be, but in the family Jennifer's in a class by herself. My dad thinks she's the big deal. They're close too, but he's closer than she is. Rosalind, what did she mean, sister *below?'*

But I was not to learn, because two customers came into the shop together, and Rosalind, with 'Can I help you?', went over to them.

'Nice tête-à-tête?' said Jennifer.

'There was no need for you to be so revoltingly arch. O-o-o, excuse Me-e!'

'I think you've fallen for her.'

'You can think what you like.'

'I wouldn't blame you if you did.'

'Actually, you sound as if you would.'

'I wouldn't care two bits,' said Jennifer angrily.

Things, my great-aunt had agreed with Rosalind, don't bring you happiness. She might almost have left us the shop just to rub this in. We were many thousands of pounds richer, and the shop began to do well as the summer came on, but we'd been happier in the old house, anticipating it all.

I was rather depressed because Rosalind had gone right back into her shell. She 'kept herself to herself' better than anyone else in the world, and I was not even sure whether or not I had fallen for her, because she didn't give me a chance to find out.

This was not the only reason, though. Jennifer hated the shop, and it conveyed itself to me. Something about it upset her. It had an atmosphere, impossible to define, but *there*, like hatred between polite people. I thought this had cleared away after our twin-dream, but to my dismay it had returned. Jennifer said nothing, but her work began to suffer. The teachers went on giving her A's from force of habit, but they hinted that the zest had gone out of her essays. Full of zest were Jennifer's essays, normally. My father was worried. We didn't go to his classes, of course, but he knew all about us. He kept glancing at Jennifer with the same expression he wore when the car went wrong.

'If he looks at me again with that dying-duck face I shall scream,' she muttered.

As it happened, she sailed through mock A Levels as expected, and also played Portia very prettily in the end of term play. I helped with the stage lighting, and after we had been congratulated by everyone for miles on having such a brilliant actress in the family, I drove the car home, my father being too excited over Jennifer to be safe at the wheel. The shop had no garage, so I dumped them, drove to the nearby one we were hiring, and came back alone.

There was a gleam of light under my bedroom door. Jennifer, I thought, waylaying me for some jittery reason of her own. And then, as I reached for the doorknob, I felt a wave of fear that surpassed anything I had ever felt before.

I opened my door from a kind of hypnotic compulsion. My room was filled with weak and sickly light. I scrabbled at the light switch and filled the room with the bright light of modern science. For the moment I felt immunized, as you do when you switch off the television. But when I looked round, and my glance passed the old fireplace on the right-hand wall between the cupboards, I saw the shape of a woman, faint in the light, with the cupboard's panelling visible through her.

I think she had her back to me, but she was very indistinct. I recorded to myself, slowly and deliberately, as if explaining to a foreigner, 'I am looking at the ghost of my great-aunt. She is haunting the shop.'

She became much clearer, into focus, as it were, like a slide projected on a screen. She turned and faced me. The shock was that she was young.

She wore a frock that flattened her figure and gave her a boyish, rather oblong look. She was milky-white with the glow of after death, but I could make out the bobbed hair and the pert 'flapper' face, and if she had not been a ghost she would have looked the very opposite of the usual idea of one. She was the picture of nineteen-twenties chic, but totally out of keeping with this bright-young-thing look was her expression: distressed, bewildered, little-girl-lost. She was like some child film star forced into sophistication far beyond its years and yearning hopelessly to be allowed to be a child.

I was very, very frightened. The dead are terrifying. And yet I willed her to stay there, and with all my might I strove to make her speak to me. But my strength was not enough, and neither was hers. A weak, pitiful moan came from her mouth, and then she faded out, leaving me staring at the cupboard door, and so drained of strength that I felt like a ghost myself.

I left my light on and lay on my bed fully dressed. At first I was sure that Jennifer would come in. The current must have been irresistible. Then it occurred to me that she might be too frightened to do so, and I was ready to risk my father's displeasure by going in to her. And then my instinct told me that this time the current had not worked at all, and that Jennifer was not in communication with me, and knew nothing about this, and was, in all probability, asleep.

My head spun. I had no power of reasoning left. And after this I either passed out or fell naturally asleep; but as I did so one idea reeled in my brain; that ghostly visitation had not been intended for me; it had been intended for my sister; and somehow I had managed to deflect it.

CHAPTER THREE

The summer holidays began, and now Rosalind worked in the shop full time. Not that I got any closer to her. My mother was with her most of the time. She had really taken to Rosalind. She would ruffle her hair affectionately when she passed her in the shop.

'Mum's gained a daughter,' said Jennifer rather sourly.

'Well, don't be greedy. How many eyes do you want to be the apple of?'

'Dad thinks he adores me,' said Jennifer, 'but he doesn't, he idealizes me. He loves someone he's made up himself. He doesn't know anything about me. He'd get a shock if he did. I envy that Rosalind.'

'*Envy* her?'

'Yes, she's going to be a nurse, isn't she? Well, that's a marvellous thing to be. She'll make a fantastic one.'

'But, Jen, you'll have a fabulous career.'

'Oh, John, I'm so sick of all this front-running. "You'll take A Levels in your stride, Jenny." You'll take a degree in your stride, Jenny. Then you'll take something else, Jenny. And after that something else. He hovers over me as if I were a puppet and he were working the strings.'

'Oh, fair play, with the best intentions.'

'Well, of course he has good intentions. That's just it. I know I should be grateful and I feel so guilty because I'm not.'

I said, tentatively, 'How do you feel about this house now?'

'Oh, I'm coping,' said Jennifer, in a tone that suggested that she wasn't coping at all.

Rosalind was coping all right. She spoke politely to my mother when she was spoken to, but she never volunteered a remark. I found her quiet, self-contained ways very provocative. Once or twice she gave me her own peculiar look, half come-on and half keep-off, but as I was not to know which half would come up if I tried getting friendly, I held back, and it seemed that we'd go on in this way for ever.

Meanwhile, not five minutes of any day passed but I saw it again in my mind: a thin white shape turning to face me: not a gaunt old woman but a young girl. I would brood on it till the young face melted through its features like a dissolving cloud.

As I was helping her in the shop one afternoon, Rosalind remarked:

'You look sad.'

'Do I?' I said glumly.

'Yes. You shouldn't.'

'You mean I'm so lucky having parents and a sister? You don't keep on thinking you're lucky, just because–'

'You should do.'

'Count my blessings, like?'

'Yes.'

'Well, as for that,' I said, 'I haven't really got a father, I've got the president of the Jennifer fan-club. Surely you've noticed that?'

'But that's the *point*. You've got *someone* to have a grudge against, and *someone* to be jealous of, and that. They're *yours*.'

She was flushed, and actually trembling. I knew that I had to speak up now, before she went all aloof again.

'There's someone I haven't got,' I said.

I was stammering and my heart was pounding. I said things I had never dreamed I could say. Rosalind watched me sternly.

She said, low and urgent, 'You're not just saying all this, are you?'

'Rosalind–'

She relented a little. 'But you're in a state to say anything.'

'Rosalind, I–'

An open shop is not the ideal place for this sort of discussion. Whatever I was about to say or do next was cut short by the entry of a lady who was looking for paperweights, and examined every single one we had, and she was really taken with two of them, but she was buying for a friend, you see, and she'd have to ask her about it, and went away, leaving Rosalind to put the fifty-odd of them back in their cases.

It gave me a chance to get my second wind, however.

'Rosalind,' I said, 'I need you. I really do, this is not just the routine boloney. I've got a problem, and my family can't help.'

'So you only want to make use of me?'

She was teasing, actually. 'Yes, that's right,' I said.

For at least the second time in her life, she smiled. 'O.K.,' she said. 'What can I do?'

'You must know much more about the old lady and the shop than any of us. Well, it is haunted. There's a ghost. No, listen. Please.'

Rosalind listened reluctantly. She was like a grown-up trying to avoid telling the facts of life to some kid. She made excuses. She said that the eerie glow could have been from the dress-shop opposite, whose light stayed on all night. She said that the curtains might look like a ghostly figure in the gloom. When I told her how Jennifer had scared me as a child, she seized on it.

'She planted ideas in your head.'

'She gave herself some, too.'

'Yes, but she passes her fears on to you. You two are tremendously close.'

'I saw a ghost. Not a trick of the light. Not a thought-transmission. A ghost. There was always something funny about this place, wasn't there?'

'I never saw anything.'

'Or heard anything?'

' . . . No.'

'Why do you hesitate?'

'I think . . . I think *she* did.'

'Try to remember all you can about her.'

'But it wasn't her you saw. She wasn't a young girl.'

'No, but what I saw may have been what she used to talk to. Rosalind, why are you so reluctant?'

'I don't *know*,' she exclaimed, piteously.

'Well, it's misplaced loyalty. Look, she's dead. We saw her cremated. I'm alive, and you can't expect me to go on seeing the ghost of some girl in my bedroom without taking some interest in it.'

'No, all right, John . . . Look, I'll tell you what. We'll look through my album.'

The next afternoon, early closing day, I 'took Rosalind out'. It was my family's expression, not mine. If anyone was taken out, I was, because we went first to the Rainham Foundation and then to a teashop of Rosalind's choosing. My parents evidently approved. My mother went about humming to herself; then at the last moment she went all serious. 'You mind you treat her properly, now, John.'

'All right,' I said, not sure quite what to make of that.

'That little girl takes things very seriously.'

'All right, Mum,' I said. I didn't much like Rosalind being called 'a little girl', but she was right enough about the seriousness.

My father was oddly pleased. He even lent me his new car. 'So she's going to show you her photograph album, is she? In my day it used to be etchings.'

Jennifer looked at me quizzically.

'If you raise your eyebrows any higher,' I said, 'you'll catch them in your hair.'

'Don't do anything I wouldn't do.'

Rosalind led me across the lawns of the Rainham Foundation and left me for a few minutes in the Visitors' Lounge. I suspected that behind the closed door all the girls in the Home were piled up, so that it must soon burst open and pour an avalanche of them into the room. There was a rustling and scuffling, like rats in the walls. Someone whispered, *'Seen* him,' and a chorus answered, 'Sh-sh!' Rosalind returned in a cream blouse and trousers bought with her new wages, and we crossed the lawns again. Groups of girls were now dotted about the grounds. They greeted Rosalind with studied casualness. I guessed they'd talk about nothing else all day. I felt flattered to arouse so much interest, but guilty too, in a way. They were like prisoners seeing one of their number released.

But oh! Annabel's Teashop, and Rosalind beside me! We sat on a window-ledge seat. It was shady and cool. Outside the village street was white like lime in the sun. I was besotted with her. But she produced the album, calm and businesslike.

It was an old-fashioned, strongly-made one, with padded covers. There were photos in sepia which went well back into the last century. We turned the pages until we reached my great-aunt's own generation, some sixty years back. There were tennis-club photos, a wedding or two, and various ones of girls in shortish skirts with the waistline around the hips, and Cleopatra fringes, and hats like coal-scuttles. We couldn't tell for certain if my great-aunt herself was one of them, the old woman we had known had been so withered by time. We turned another page.

'They went in for slave-bangles a lot, didn't they?' murmured Rosalind.

But I started out of my moony haze.

'That's her!'

It was a young girl in a long white gown, very actressy. Her hands were clasped under her chin, and her face was tilted soulfully upward.

'This one? Are you sure? Who is it? Miss Crawley when she was young?'

Rosalind slipped the photo from the page and looked at the back of it.

'Alice, as Desdemona, Strolling Players, June 1923. That's Shakespeare, isn't it? Her name wasn't Alice.'

'No, Clara. Alice was her sister, I think.'

'You think? Your family, and you don't know?'

'Well, she died. Ages ago.'

'Ask your mother about her.'

'This is Dad's side of the family, not Mum's.'

'Yes, but I bet your mum knows more about it.'

I asked both parents. Neither knew much. They had both been born seventeen years after Alice's death, and Great-Aunt Clara never spoke about her. I learned that Alice had died when she was only twenty-three, less than a year after that photo was taken, and that her mother, a widow, was so grieved that she never recovered; in fact she had to go into a mental home, where soon afterwards she died. Not long after this, Clara converted their house into a shop.

'You seem very interested,' said my mother. 'It all comes from seeing her picture, does it?'

'He didn't want to see it at all, poor chap,' said my father, 'but there were so many people about that he and his inamorata were compelled to look at the album after all.'

'Isn't it amazing,' I said to Rosalind later, 'that they seem to have absolutely no idea that they might walk into Alice on the landing? Do you know, I think this ghost haunts special people only. Jennifer. I'm sure it was looking for Jennifer. Why should it want Jennifer?'

'Hoping to join the fan-club, perhaps. No, sorry, that wasn't nice. After Jennifer? Well, now that I've heard about Alice, I reckon she was around long before Jennifer came into it. I think it was her your auntie used to talk to.'

'"My sister below".'

'That's right. And when I thought she was watching for burglars and that, she was–'

'Looking out for Alice?'

'That's right.'

'A right mystery, this, isn't it?'

'You can say that again. And I was taught there's no such things as ghosts.'

From this time on we pried into every corner of the shop, looking for anything, old letters or diaries, that might throw light on the family. In the basement there were several boxes with old magazines and papers in them. As soon as we got the chance Rosalind and I went down there on the pretext of tidying up, and began the dusty job of examining their contents.

The dolls stared vacantly at me. The birch-broom collected cobwebs in its cupboard. There was no 'atmosphere' down here. I am rather ashamed to admit that I was more interested in being alone with Rosalind than I was in the search. But she was absorbed in it, and kept turning out the junk with the mechanical persistence of a creature building its lair.

She drew out a bundle of what looked like old cuttings-books, and began turning the pages of one. Newspaper cuttings, cookery recipes in handwriting, bits of verse. All yellow-brown with age.

She looked up suddenly.

'There's–'

There was atmosphere now all right.

'There's something here. With us.'

'Yes,' I said hoarsely. 'Let's get out.'

She hesitated.

'Rosalind!'

'No.'

I took her wrist and tried to pull her away. She freed herself and shook her head.

'No. You go.'

She began to say something more. But just then the telephone, the old one with the useless flex, began ringing like mad.

Yes, it was this telephone all right, not a normal one somewhere else creating a delusion; it was this one, with its little hammer quivering between the bells. Rosalind crept up to it and stood with her hand hovering above the receiver.

'For God's sake don't touch it,' I implored her. 'You don't know what it is. Leave it, leave it.'

She lifted the receiver and held it to her ear.

There was a second receiver, a small round one, on the other side of the instrument. I held it to my ear, putting my free arm around her waist and holding her tight. A voice was speaking on this dead line, so feebly and so far away that we could not make out the words; but it was a female voice, tremulous with age.

'*Miss Crawley*,' said Rosalind.

The weak, bodiless whisper grew more urgent, but still it was impossible to make sense of it.

'Miss Crawley, it's Rosalind. I'm listening.'

But it died hopelessly away.

Rosalind turned and clung to me and buried her face in my shoulder.

'Come on, sit down,' I said.

'That was an old voice,' I said.

'It was her voice,' said Rosalind. 'Clara's.'

CHAPTER FOUR

My father now dropped a bomb. We were to go on holiday in Italy. Jennifer needed to get away from it all. 'It all', needless to say, didn't include himself. Of course, we had not been on holiday with our parents for years – it is something no-one over the age of twelve should do – but this fell on us with the swiftness of a mugging, and we had not time to make other arrangements. In an unusual burst of efficiency he arranged for us to leave almost at once. Money helped; no package tour this time: a posh hotel by Lake Garda.

I hoped briefly that I might be left behind with Rosalind, but the Rainham would soon have tracked that down and stopped it – they were naturally careful with the girls – and anyway, my mother would not let me fend for myself for a fortnight. I was cornered. I'll say it for my father, he tried hard to console me.

'Sorry about this, old chap. I realize you've got a strong incentive to stay behind. Never mind, she'll still be here when you come back! The fact is, I dare not take the car abroad without my co-driver.'

Rosalind was right when she said that being nice doesn't mean anything.

'I'll write to you,' I told her despondently.

'I expect I'll get it about a week after you come back.'

'Will you miss me?'

'Oh, no, of course not.'

'Listen, promise me you won't do any investigating while I'm away. That phone call scared me stiff. Promise.'

'All right.'

'Promise!'

'I have, haven't I?'

I'd never been more fed up in my life. We went on trips which involved zonking over the tarmac strips of motorways for countless miles and then being led in herds round boring places by tip-hungry guides. We hired a motorboat. We swam in the hotel pool. We danced after dinner.

But luckily our parents ran out of energy more quickly than my sister and I, and would sink into chairs outside cafés and drink capuccino, and this gave us the chance to get away alone. I had to tell Jennifer what had been happening. If I didn't she'd learn for herself and get a shock. I rowed her far out across the lake and we talked; or rather she asked the questions and I cautiously answered them. I stuck to the bare facts. I didn't tell her that I thought Alice's ghost had been looking for her. She gulped a bit when she heard the spooky details, but she was relieved not to be in the dark any more.

'Golly,' she said, 'our esteemed great-aunts should have been called the Creepy Crawleys . . . Why have you been hiding all this?'

'Afraid of scaring you, I suppose.'

'Fit for Rosalind, though, wasn't it? . . . Well, well. So we heard Alice and Clara in my dream, did we? Yes, of course, who else? Talk about Rest in Peace. So who's been haunting whom?'

I shook my head. Jennifer hunched up in her end of the boat, pale under her tan.

'I reckon Rosalind's the cause of all this,' she said at last.

'Don't be ridiculous. This is a family thing.'

'It's not. Why haven't Mum and Dad seen or heard anything?'

'Dad only sees things in books.'

'No, he's a bundle of nerves. If he were meant to be haunted

36

he'd know all right. It's *us*. And Rosalind's not only in on the act, she's the leading lady.'

'You mean she's some sort of medium?'

'I don't know what mediums are. I do know that Rosalind is absolutely crazy about families and would do anything to kid herself that she belonged to one. And according to you, Clara thought a hell of a lot of her, which is more than she did of us. She despised us. What I'm saying is that Rosalind and she were very very close, and that now she's dead Rosalind could be a sort of contact for her. If that makes Rosalind a medium, she's a medium.'

In a glum and vacant way I watched the stern of our boat gently rising and falling against the line of the shore.

'I reckon she projected that dream on to me,' said Jennifer.

'What, before you even met her?'

'She saw me at the funeral.'

'For God's sake, Jen.'

'Sorry, John. I know you're very fond of her.'

'I know you bloody well aren't.'

'Oh, I like her very much.'

While we were away Rosalind kept her promise and did not 'investigate', but she did keep looking through the album. The odd thing was that there were no photos of Clara. There were plenty of Alice: Alice at six months lying on a cushion; Alice as a three-year-old ballerina, curtseying; Alice as Wendy in *Peter Pan*; Alice (fully grown) in Shakespearian and modern roles. The old-fashioned photos showed that Alice had been very pretty, with dimples and great big eyes that implored the world to be gentle with her.

'Spoiled,' said Rosalind. She recalled the angular old woman, Clara, and tried to imagine her as a girl. 'Plain, maybe. Or thought she was. Camera-shy.'

Something occurred to her. When Clara had given her the album, she had said, 'All the people in this are now at peace, except one, and she soon will be.' Rosalind had assumed that Clara meant herself, soon to die. But she couldn't have done, because she wasn't in the album at all.

'She meant Alice, then? I wonder what was between them?'

On Sundays, when the shop was closed, Rosalind did voluntary work at an Old People's Home nearby. She talked to them and walked them in the grounds and sometimes took them for drives in an estate car which the Home entrusted her to use. Mrs Waltham of the Rainham Foundation had told everyone that Rosalind liked difficult cases, and so her latest charge was a fearful old woman named Elsie, who wrote poison-pen notes to the other inmates, calling them *sneeks* and *cheets*. She always greeted Rosalind with a snarl: 'Who are you? Don't know you. Don't want to.' Rosalind would talk her round and would accept the poisonous notes, which she then dropped into a waste-paper bin outside. This Sunday she was caught doing it.

'The best place for them, my dear,' said an ancient voice. 'She invents it all, you know.'

'She's old.'

'Oh! eighty-three,' said the lady, from her wheel-chair. 'I don't call that old. I'm eighty-nine myself.'

Rosalind feigned astonishment and began a polite conversation, but the old lady wasn't listening. She was staring at Rosalind with great interest. She said:

'You're the young lady who works at Crawleys! I thought I'd seen you before. I've passed the shop once or twice when people have taken me out, you know. Oh, I have wanted to go inside!'

'Whyever didn't you?'

'No, no, I should have wasted your time, I should have talked the hind leg off a donkey . . . That place has so many memories for me, you see. I was in service to the Crawley family long before it was a shop . . . Well, I went there when I was thirteen–that will tell you how long ago it was . . .'

'Did you know Alice and Clara?'

'Know them! I should think I did!'

'Would you like me to take you there?'

'Oh, I should love it! But such trouble for you–'

'No problem,' said Rosalind. She watched her as though afraid she might fade away, like Alice.

'Not more than an hour, then, Rosalind,' said the matron. 'She must not get overtired.'

The old lady, Mrs Porter, called Rosalind Rosemary and sometimes Renée, but she remembered her youth in detail. She gazed round our new home delightedly.

'This wasn't always a shop, you know . . . This was the front parlour and that glass door wasn't there . . .'

She had married sixty-three years before, and had lived in London till three months ago. When her husband died she had returned to the Cotswolds to live with a niece, but her arthritis had got worse and she had had to enter the Old People's Home.

'But I can walk if you take it slowly.'

Slowly it was. They crawled through the house, Mrs Porter dwelt nostalgically on every part of it, and Rosalind's hour was slipping away. At last they returned to the shop and descended by creaking inches to the basement.

'Ah, the dolls! Miss Clara loved her dolls! No-one must touch her dolls! She could be spiteful to them, mind. When she was cross with Miss Alice she would smack them and stick pins in them!'

'Was she often cross with–'

'Oh, she did love her dolls! Her greatest punishment was to be forbidden to play with them!'

'Was she often cross with–'

'She did so love her dolls!'

'She wouldn't sell them,' said Rosalind. 'She always made excuses not to.'

'What did you say, Rosemary?'

'She would never sell–'

'No, you said, was she cross with her sister. Ah, yes, I'm afraid she was, and it was such a shame, because Miss Alice was such a pretty little thing . . . Jealous, you know . . . Many times I wanted to scold her, but it was not my place . . .'

Rosalind was a good listener, and she listened.

The mother of the two girls had been a small-time actress who had married the heir to a title, but he had been killed in the First World War before coming into it. As a widow, comfortably off, Mrs Crawley had devoted the rest of her life to persuading Alice that she was a great actress, and the best singer and dancer, and the prettiest girl in the world with it.

'Some people thought she made rather too much of it, but it was understandable in a mother, wasn't it?'

'Did Alice become a professional actress?'

No, Mrs Crawley had played safe. Alice remained an amateur.

'Such a pretty little thing, and so modest. She used to say, "I wish Mother wouldn't make such a fuss. I'm not nearly as good as she thinks I am . . ." I think she got very tired. She was always rehearsing for some play or other . . . Sometimes it made her seem quite unhappy, although goodness knows she had everything to be thankful for . . . until her sad illness, of course . . .

'And then Miss Clara did that dreadful thing . . .'

'What dreadful thing?'

'Oh, I wasn't supposed to know, of course . . . But of course, it was a dreadful shock, and I believe it was that turned poor Mrs Crawley's mind . . .'

'Mrs Porter! What did Miss Clara do?'

'Of course, she was always jealous. Do you know, when they were children, Miss Clara once wrote "I HATE MY

SISTER" in chalk on the pavement outside, where all the neighbours could see it!'

'Did she? Oh dear. Mrs Porter, what was it that–?'

'It is getting very close in here, Renée.'

'Mrs Porter, what–?'

'I think I should like to go up now . . .'

'Yes, of course,' said Rosalind resignedly. She was a born nurse. The old lady must not be over-excited. She helped her upstairs.

'So kind . . . I'm afraid I've been talking too much . . .'

Much too much, and not enough. Rosalind repeated her question, strategically, several times on the way back, but got no answer that made sense. Oh well, it would come out in the end. She couldn't bring her to the shop again, as we would be back by the next Saturday, but she could talk to her in the Home.

She returned to her own clinically white little room at the Rainham, sat on the edge of her bed, and trembled.

Dreadful thing?

She had adopted Great-Aunt Clara, and she felt like a tigress with its young. She had adopted her because she herself was a girl of no identity, named after a street. She wished to hear no evil of her.

Her mind ranged from murder to grave-robbing.

'She was all right,' she muttered, 'Crabby, but she'd never have hurt anyone.'

Ah, but sixty years back? In the heat of youth?

'She'd not hurt anyone,' repeated Rosalind sullenly.

The next Tuesday (guesswork had decided) was Rosalind's birthday. She was eighteen, three months older than I. There were seventy-one girls at the Rainham, so that birthdays came round rather often, but none went unnoticed. The birthday girl got a shower of cards from staff and girls, and a cake which was shared round at tea-time. Rosalind also got cards from us, left with Mrs Waltham before we went on holiday: one from my parents (signed by my father, but chosen by my mother), one from Jennifer, and one from me. I decided at the last moment against a sexy jokey one, and sent her a safe boring one with a picture by an R.A.

Everyone liked birthday teas, and the lovely iced cake with the name on it, but Rosalind didn't seem to be enjoying this one much. Mrs Waltham ran an eye over her, reflected that she had got herself a boy-friend and was crazy about families, and took her aside.

'Under the weather, Ros?'

'No, I'm all right.'

'You'd tell me if anything were wrong, wouldn't you? Because naturally we like to know in time.'

'I'm all right.'

'And that's a fact?'

'Yes, that's a proven fact.'

'Ah! Good, good. Just making sure, that's all. I was afraid my cake had done for you.'

Rosalind went to her room to write thank-you notes to my parents and Jennifer, but she felt unable to attend to the simplest action. When she put up her cards about her room, a thing she normally loved doing, she could hardly bring herself to finish. Reluctantly, even with distaste, she got out her notepaper and sat at her table. She wrote her address and the date.

But she could not concentrate. She had felt like this ever since taking Mrs Porter to the shop; it was as if, she told me, she were literally 'not herself'; as if she were being manipulated, like a puppet. She began writing, but it was not herself writing, nor was her own mind directing it. Her hand moved across the paper of its own will.

At the same time, curiously, she was able to think about what was happening.

Clara was guiding her hand.

The influence lost power and died. Rosalind was sure that she was about to learn what Clara wanted of her. She looked at the notepaper. The address, the date, were in her own handwriting. She looked for the message.

There was no message; there was only a squiggly line, like an electronic graph. There were peaks and dips, but no words. Clara's spirit, like any living person, seemed to be having trouble making itself understood.

CHAPTER FIVE

I don't think my father enjoyed his holiday overmuch. For one thing, the hotel was too grand. He could afford it for a fortnight, but it brought him into the company of really rich people, Swedes and Germans and Americans, with their binoculars and cameras and boats and their air of living like this all the time, and I think it made him feel inferior. For another, he was put out because I had monopolized Jennifer. Guests at the hotel remarked on what good friends we were. 'Aren't you lucky! Our two fight like cat and dog!' This didn't please him. It would be hard to say what would have pleased him. He wanted everyone to admire Jennifer, and was affronted when they did. I was sorry for any boy-friend she might get.

He didn't admit any of this, of course. He was determined that the holiday should be a success.

'Jenny looks much better, doesn't she?'

'Yes, dear.'

'It's done her the world of good!'

'Yes. John's caught the sun a bit too, hasn't he?'

My mother kept us all in order. I couldn't possibly say how. She did it by doing nothing. I could never confide in her, though. I always felt that, if I got past the serenity and tackled her closely, I should find nothing there.

'Everyone puts on an act,' said my cynical sister, when I mentioned this. 'Everyone does. It's what keeps them going.'

We got back home late on the Saturday evening. Rosalind

rang the next morning. She'd found out some things about the Crawley family, she told me. And something mysterious had happened. But look, don't get cross, but she *had* to go to the Old People's Home today.

Don't get cross! I had been pining for Rosalind for two weeks, and already I was losing my temper.

'Oh, do you have to?'

'I'll explain when I see you.'

'Explain now.'

'No, there's someone waiting outside this phone box. 'Bye!'

How could she stay so calm? She couldn't love me as much as I loved her. Superficial, she was. I worked myself into a boiling rage. I was then overcome with remorse. I then felt depleted and doleful. I used up about as much energy as I would have done running a marathon, and all, more or less, without moving from the spot.

Meanwhile Rosalind, with Mrs Porter in mind, and with a score of questions cunningly prepared, went to the Old People's Home.

'Mrs Porter?' said the sister in charge. 'Oh, Rosalind, I'm so sorry, but she's had a stroke . . . Last Thursday . . . Well, at her age, pretty serious, I'm afraid . . . Oh, no, not your fault, of course not . . . Well, we all are, very sorry . . . I'm afraid these things happen, you know . . . Anyway, I'm sure Elsie's looking forward to seeing you . . .'

'A last year's Volvo,' I said. 'Estate car. A beauty. That Home must think a lot of her, mustn't they, to let her–'

'Oh, *everyone* thinks a lot of Rosalind,' said Jennifer. 'She's everyone's sweetheart, Little Orphan Annie. John, I'm sorry, but it's true. You, Mum, that Waltham woman, they all drool over Rosalind. Even old hag Clara did. And why? Because she's got everything going for her! She looks like the Virgin Mary, she's sweet, she's good, and she was found on a doorstep. What more do you want?'

45

'I suppose she'd be luckier still if she lost a leg.'

'You simply do not understand.'

'What is there to understand?'

Jennifer burst into tears.

'Jen . . . ?'

'Now you've made me cry,' said Jennifer furiously, 'and it's so degrading. If you tell Rosalind I cried I'll kill you.'

'I'm afraid to speak.'

Jennifer put down her shopping basket and sat down on the bench by the obelisk, at the other end of the high street from our shop.

'Perhaps you should hold me under the village pump.'

'Perhaps we should talk sense.'

'Not just go over the same thing again, no.'

We went back, carrying the heavy load of post-holiday shopping. My father was away on some teachers' conference, and Rosalind, sleeveless in the heat, and white-armed beside the rest of us, was working with my mother in the shop. When I set eyes on her I was filled with tenderness, but she didn't feel the same about me just then. Her glance flickered over us, carrying the heaviest basket between us.

'Practically Siamese,' she murmured, smiling just a little too sweetly.

'Feel the weight, chum,' said Jennifer, pretending to share the joke.

'Goodness! What a good thing there are two of you!'

She said to me later, 'Had Jennifer been crying?'

'No.'

'I really cannot see what she's got to cry about.'

'What was that crack about Siamese twins?'

'Need you ask?'

I had hoped that telling Jennifer everything would make a team of us. I suppose I'd vaguely expected us to behave like those jolly groups in stories: *Five Go Grave-robbing* kind of thing. It hadn't turned out like that at all. The girls' dislike for each other had ripened like a boil.

Mind you, you would never have guessed from their manner. They were friendlier than they had ever been. They were sickeningly friendly. They exchanged inane chit-chat and trilled with laughter. It was almost like a conspiracy. I felt out of place in this female freemasonry, as if I belonged to another species.

That evening Rosalind and I went to a disco in the village, and jumped around a bit, but without much elation. She was a good dancer, and literally made circles around me, but her expression was resigned, as if she were reluctantly dancing to order.

'Enjoying this?' I asked, when the pulsating thunder ceased for a moment.

'Well, nice not to be playing gooseberry for once.'

'Shouldn't that be Jennifer's line?'

'No. Mine.'

The music began again. I shook my head and drew her out of the hall, and we walked by the river in the delicious evening air. Our village, Mitten-on-the-Water, is short on peasants and very well up in arty-crafties on the make, and these have managed to make even the river look phoney, because they have bathed it in coloured lights to attract the tourists. Even so, Rosalind looked stunning, glowing in shifting shades of crimson and old-gold, and my purpose weakened. Nevertheless I said:

'Now, then. Why talk of playing gooseberry? Jennifer's my sister, so what could be safer than that?'

'Blood's thicker than water,' said Rosalind tritely.

'Messier, too.'

'Oh, you sound just like her. Clever. I can't say clever things like you . . . Yes, I know she's your sister. You two are practically one person . . .'

'Well, what am I supposed to do about it?'

'You can't do anything, and neither can I. It's just that I don't

47

stand a chance, that's all.'

'Whatever's that supposed to mean?'

Rosalind leaned over the parapet and brooded, while the lights from the water played over her.

'You know that dream,' she said at last.

'When we–'

'Yes. John, I know it's an awful thing to say, but I think Jennifer *made* it happen so that you had to take notice of her.'

'How could she possibly–'

'People can do anything if they will it strongly enough. They can make themselves ill. They can give themselves asthma. They can even make themselves die.'

'Just what the hell is she supposed to have willed?'

'Please don't sound so cross. I hate it when you're cross.'

'Look–'

'Please, John. Don't ask me to explain because I can't. I know she didn't know anything until you told her, but I think she, like, *draws the ghost out* without knowing it, and you're getting what she ought to be getting, because she passes it on to you.'

'Like a medium?'

'I suppose so, yes.'

Well, now I had heard the same thing from both sides, and it was so mad that neither Jennifer nor Rosalind could have made it up unaided. Our ghosts were picking teams.

Something occurred to me.

'Rosalind,' I said, 'did Clara actually offer you the shop before she died? Between ourselves now?'

'Well, she did, actually.'

'And you refused? Christ!'

'I didn't want her to think I was after her money. It would have spoiled everything.'

It was clear who Clara's favourite would be. Why Alice should pick on Jennifer was a mystery.

I seemed to be piggy-in-the-middle.

You can learn to live with anything except your own emotions. I went in dread of our ghosts, but I was resigned to it, more or less; what I couldn't adjust to was being in love. I was crazy about Rosalind, yet she annoyed me beyond reason. She annoyed me by being cheerful and chatty to my mother and the customers while I myself was feeling sombre with love. She annoyed me by saying 'Can I help you?' in the same tone every time. She annoyed me by not knowing the word 'phantasmagoria' when Jennifer used it, although I had to look it up myself. I don't know why these absurd things should have annoyed me, and I was always ashamed afterwards, but that didn't stop my moods from recurring.

We fell out over her defence of Clara.

'She was all right.'

'No, maybe she wasn't. Perhaps that's at the root of all this. What about the "dreadful thing" she did?'

'She was all right.'

'You're deliberately sentimentalizing her.'

'I just know she was all right.'

'Can't you see your attitude is entirely subjective?'

'Yes, maybe it is,' said Rosalind, in sudden temper. 'And if you didn't know a blind thing about yourself, so would yours be.'

'Oh, you know I didn't mean that, Ros–'

'Please don't call me Ros.'

I saw what Jennifer meant when she said Rosalind had advantages. You had to go extra careful with her; to hurt her would be like hitting a blind girl. But how easily hurt she was.

She wouldn't go out with me that evening. She said she had 'house duties' at the Rainham.

To prove my independence, I went out with some mates I'd been neglecting lately, but I doubt if they found me good company. I was thinking all the time of what the girls had said about each other. Perhaps it was natural that they should resent each other, up to a point, but beyond that point, I believed, they were being manipulated. Until we moved to the shop, I had believed in free will. I would have said, you can have good or bad luck, yes, but you still make your own life. Now I was not so sure. There were outside influences. And if this was happening to us, perhaps it was happening, less obviously, to everyone else in the world. It made you think.

Yet if our deceased great-aunts were influencing us, they weren't doing so with much authority. Alice had faded on me pathetically before she could speak. Clara had tried to write and had achieved only a squiggle. They seemed to be groping in the dark as much as we were. In Jennifer's dream they had managed only an agitated din. They could not, it seemed, even communicate with each other.

And now, with old Mrs Porter out of action, we had about as much chance of learning any more about them as we had of naming the Unknown Warrior.

I left my friends and walked to the bus stop. As I waited for the unpunctual last bus I ran a gloomy and mindless eye over the placards outside the nearby newsagent's. 'Wed., Thur., Fri., Sat.,' I read. 'Sandy Wilson's Bubbling Musical of the Twenties. THE BOY FRIEND. Presented by–'

I suddenly took heed.

'–Presented by *The Strolling Players.*'

Alice's dram. soc., still going, after so many years?

Of course, there couldn't possibly be anyone left who . . .

They might have kept some records, though?

Even if they had, what good would that be?

Still, we clutch at straws.

I got off at the top of the high street and began walking down. The next moment I found myself in the arms of Rosalind, appearing in a fluttering rush from nowhere and alighting on me like a dove.

'Waited till seven buses went by, haven't I?'

'I've been to Gloucester.'

'Well, I know that. Why have you been so horrible?'

'Rosalind, you said –'

'Well, you shouldn't have believed me.'

Sometimes she was even more like my sister than I was. I didn't say so, though.

CHAPTER SIX

I had decided that our affair lay in ruins, and was drunk with relief to find that it did not. I thought Rosalind took the matter much more in her stride, but not everyone thought the same. My mother said:

'You're not making her unhappy, are you?'

'No.'

'She called round last night looking very worried.'

'It's all right.'

'I hope so. She's not a person to trifle with.'

Only too true. Rosalind, in fact, was a hell of a responsibility. But I was buoyant just now; you forget the bad weather when the sun comes out.

And so, chasing the slenderest of chances, but feeling that somehow my luck had turned, I rang up the Strolling Players, and was answered by a Mr Peter Knowles, whose cultured voice so boomed through the phone that Rosalind, beside me in the phone box, heard every word.

She, by the way, was optimistic. 'Those sort of people take themselves very seriously,' she said. 'They'll keep records of everything they've ever done.'

She was right. 'Yes,' said the voice of Mr Knowles, 'we've got archives going back to 1902 – when the Society was founded. What's this in aid of?'

'I'm trying to trace a Miss Alice Crawley. She was my great-aunt.'

'Congratulations. Ha ha ha!'

'She died in 1923.'

'Rather before my time, old boy. Wouldn't you do better to ask around your own family?'

I began a lame account of the family. The great-aunts were dead. Their brother, my father's father, had spent his time in prep school, public school, and the Army, had led a separate life, and was dead too. There was one picture of him in the album, aged about nine, wearing a sailor suit. Rosalind gently took the earpiece away from me.

'It's like this, Mr Knowles. We've got to do a project, and we've decided to do one on the Strolling Players, because they're, like, an important group in the community. John's related to Alice Crawley and he'd like to, like, build it round her . . .'

I was shocked by this fibbing, because my standard for Rosalind (no matter what I did myself) would have been hard for a saint to live up to, and it could have set off one of my bad moods, had it not so immediately charmed Mr Knowles.

'Oh, I *see!* Well . . .'

We called on him half an hour later that same evening. In the daytime, it seemed, he worked in an insurance office. Outside office hours he acted the part of actor-manager. He was on the phone when we arrived. We were shown in by his son, about our own age, who looked at us with bored contempt, which he seemed to feel for his father too; but Mr Knowles was so wrapped up in his role that he probably wouldn't have noticed if his son had brought in a blunderbuss and fired a shower of old nails at him.

'M'm . . . yup . . . Oh, *very* easy on the eye, yup . . . Trouble is, she can't *act*, old boy . . . No *range* . . . '

We stood humbly just inside the door, and waited for him to finish.

'*Well!* he said, throwing back his mane of iron-grey hair, and running his eyes over Rosalind in a way that suggested that he would like to do the same with his hands. 'I *say!* Hal*lo!*'

The Strolling Players had their own theatre, although it was used some of the time as a Scout Hut. The susceptible Mr Knowles took us there in his car. The walls were covered with photographs and playbills, and in the inner office were steel filing cabinets full of old programmes, newspaper cuttings, and letters.

'Well, there you are, and the best of British. I'll be around for a couple of hours because we've got a rehearsal, so if you can stand the din you're welcome . . . You can't take anything away, you understand . . . we could photo-copy for you if you care to pay for it . . . '

He fetched out some photograph albums and books of cuttings, and after leaning over Rosalind for a rather long time he left us to it.

We plodded through dozens of black and white pictures of moon-faced Edwardian actresses and gents in boaters until we came to Alice's era. There were several photos of her, but we'd seen them all before in Clara's album.

'Interesting, that,' I remarked. 'If she hated her sister, it didn't stop her collecting pictures of her.'

'You can hate someone and love them at the same time.'

I wished she wouldn't come out with these clichés. All the same, clichés are true. That's why they become clichés.

The newspaper cuttings were mainly reviews of shows, and discussed people we didn't know or care about. They contained plenty of press-photos of full casts smirking on stage. Alice could be spotted in one or two of them. And then we found a special one.

Clara was in it.

Strolling Players Win Drama Festival.

There were seven people in the picture, with Alice beaming like a bride in the middle. On the extreme left was the producer, a woman, looking like a hen proud of its brood. Then the cast of five: a man, a girl, Alice, another girl, another man, and then, extreme right, Clara: 'Miss Clara Crawley, who designed and made the costumes.'

Both Rosalind and I had always assumed that Clara had been plain, and jealous of her sister's beauty. She was not. The picture was a good one on shiny paper. She was not a Twenties mod. like Alice; she wore a mid-calf-length dress and her hair was coiled in earphones, but in her own way she was very attractive, and she looked as if she knew it, with a smile like royalty opening a bazaar. Rosalind was fascinated.

'Shows you what age can do to a person, doesn't it?'

'I'd never have recognized her.'

'Except the smile. She kept a lovely smile.'

'For you, then. We never saw it.'

'Don't be so nasty about her. Look, can you imagine her doing "a dreadful thing"?'

'Shouldn't be taken in by a pretty face,' I said darkly. I meant this, in some obscure way, to be a dig at Rosalind herself, but she didn't catch on.

'Do you notice something about this picture?'

I couldn't till she pointed it out, but then it became obvious. Everyone in the picture was posed to look round at Alice – except Clara; she broke up the pattern. She was smiling up at the man beside her.

'"Mr Basil Hunter",' read out Rosalind. He was in harlequin's costume, and tall, with hair like black glass. Like the rest, he was smiling at Columbine in the middle, and Clara's smile was catching him in the region of his left ear.

'Could be there was a man in it?' said Rosalind.

'That's guessing rather a lot.'

'If she was supposed to hate her sister, why did she make her costume for her? This number,' said Rosalind, indicating the flounces above Alice's delectable knees, 'would have been a lot of hard work, I can tell you.'

'She made costumes for them all.'

'Yes, right. For him, too. And that made it worth it. Look how she's smiling at him.'

'That's all very clever,' I said, 'but why are there no photos of Basil in her own album?'

But the cast had been gathering for rehearsal on the other side of the wall. A piano began tinkling and jumping. 'It's never too late to fall in love,' quacked a quavery male voice, and a baby-squeak responded: 'Boop-a-doop, boop-a-doop, boop-a-doop!' Mr Knowles looked in at us.

'Deafening you?'

'Could we come again, Mr Knowles?'

'Peter, darling. Yes, of course you can.'

We went out into the hall and watched the rehearsal from the back for a while. Mr Knowles interrupted at times to say, 'Careful not to mask her, old boy,' and 'Ham this bit up, darling. You just can't overdo it,' and so on. Jennifer had said, 'Everyone puts on an act. It's what keeps them going.' Mr Knowles was certainly absorbed in his, and I thought of his son and wondered what ill ease lay beneath it. I'd taken a liking to him, in spite of his tentative passes at Rosalind. He was a kind-hearted man.

I saw Rosalind home–although she was now the Rainham's oldest inhabitant she still had to keep to hours–and decided to walk back to kill time. As I got into the rhythm of the walk I thought about Clara, over and over again in time with my strides: the smiling girl in the picture, and the embittered old one we had known, who had held conversations with the dead. The 'dreadful thing' she was said to have done. Her local reputation as a witch.

And if we all put on an act, what did her last one cover up?

The high street was deserted when I finally walked down it, and our shop was in darkness, with the light from the dress-shop reflecting in its window behind the metal grill. I halted in front of it for a moment. My black silhouette was picked out on the glass.

And then in the next instant my outline was no longer there, but filled with the figure of Great-Aunt Clara, gaunt and

56

haggard as we had seen her in life, and terrible-eyed.

We were separated by not more than two feet. I expected her to stab a finger at me, as she had been used to do to passers-by, and if she had done so I think I should have passed out. My mouth went dry and my skin went cold and the fear of death was on me. She was looking not at me but through me. I could see through her: the dark objects in the shop behind her showed through her whiteness like blotches on a satellite weather chart. Then her eyes moved in their hollow sockets and fixed on me. Her mouth moved. But then her whole body began to move, to shimmer and dissolve. The agony in her face as this happened was indescribable. For all my terror I wanted to hold her there, steady, as I had wanted to retain the image of Alice.

But it was no good. It was one more sickening and terrifying failure. The next moment I faced nothing but my own silhouette. I leaned against the window for a few seconds and then stumbled round to our house door and let myself in.

CHAPTER SEVEN

Jennifer was being awful to my father; not rude, but like ice. It made him feel guilty. 'Just where did I go wrong?' he kept muttering, in brooding asides, like some Shakespearean actor. *Anything* Jennifer did, in his view, was on his account. He was a good teacher and he knew quite well how ambitious parents can drive their kids too far, and he dreaded doing the same himself. But also, in a blind sort of way, he blamed me. He thought that I turned Jennifer against him. He never said so, but he harboured a grudge against me. It showed in stupid bits of sarcasm.

'In rather late, aren't you?'

'Been putting the car away, haven't I?'

'"Bin putt'n' the car away, en-I?"' he repeated, sighing disgustedly, and walked off. I could have crowned him. Yet I felt sorry for him in a way.

Jennifer and Rosalind were wearing me down between them. They went on being nice to each other with such deadly sweetness that I was almost afraid to leave them alone together. And this made me feel a traitor to each of them. I ought to decide whose side I was on, but I was on both.

The current between Jennifer and me had never been so strong. Rosalind sensed this. She kept asking me what I was thinking about. Then, when I made excuses, she would pretend that I had snubbed her. 'Sorry to be so inquisitive!' At the best of times, it was never possible to discuss the current, because it couldn't be put into words; but these were the worst of times, because Jennifer was stalling on me.

I mean that she was dreaming, night after night. I knew she was and she knew that I knew, but I couldn't share her dreams, because she was stalling on me. She was dreaming in despite of me. She went around with a small secret look. Nothing, if she could help it, would be filtered through to Rosalind.

I couldn't discuss this with Rosalind nor, of course, with my parents. They were the last people on earth with whom I could discuss anything. Outside home, even their presence embarrassed me. School functions, open days, and the like, were a misery. Apart from that, they were extraordinarily ignorant of what was going on, and it would hardly have been fair to have told them. They had worries enough as it was. Moving house is always a strain and our move had not been as happy as they had hoped for. My father chewed the cud like Hamlet over it. 'Just *where* did I go wrong?' He didn't know the half of it.

But my mother did. Half of it, that is. The human half.

She said to me, out of the blue. 'You're rather up against things just now, aren't you?'

Then, as I stared at her, 'Well, don't lose your nerve. They both draw strength from you, you know.'

She had a way of saying mysterious things straight out of her unconscious. No good asking her what she meant, because she didn't know herself.

She ruffled my hair, in that way of hers.

She had boosted my morale considerably, because I was feeling very uneasy about both girls. 'Drew strength from me!'

So, when Jennifer and I were on our next shopping trip – this was a family chore – I sat down on the seat by the obelisk and played the bullying brother. I gripped her wrist hard.

'You got something to tell me?'

'Yes, you're hurting my wrist.'

'Jen, come on.'

She looked at me with a sidelong glance. Then she turned

and looked at me squarely.

'John, are you feeling all right?'

No, I was not. I had gone white. For a split second I had been looking at the face of Alice.

An illusion, of course. But the family likeness was amazing. She was just like that stricken soul I had seen in my bedroom. There was the same cuteness, the same aren't-I-clever air; and underneath, the same quite pathetic plea for sympathy.

'I'm all right,' I said. 'What has Alice been telling you?'

She stopped stalling and gave in.

'She's not *told* me anything. She doesn't *tell*. I've never seen her or heard her. She transmits feeling. I know just how she felt.'

'And how did she feel?'

'Guilty.'

'What about?'

'Hatred.'

'Jen, this isn't a quiz game. Who hated who? Clara hated her, you mean?'

'Oh, no, no. Oh well, yes. Clara hated her all right. It's easy to hate someone like Alice. It's all very well for Rosalind to be kind to doddering old women. The hard thing is to like people like me. Oh yes, Clara hated Alice. And Alice was more or less forced into making Clara hate her.'

'How come?'

'Because people act as they're expected to. They don't know they're doing it at first, and when they realize it, it's too late, they've moulded themselves. But I don't want to go on about Clara.'

'So Alice hated someone?'

'Yes. Her mother.'

Bit by bit—rather like a psychiatrist with a patient, I should think—I got Jennifer to explain. Alice had hated her mother, and had felt terribly guilty about it, because her mother had given her everything. She had spoiled her in every sense of the word. She had never let her be herself. She had made her play the role of Alice the great actress, Alice the beauty queen, Alice the all-round wonder girl. If Alice protested, her mother simply added another virtue – Alice was sweetly modest and didn't think enough of herself. Alice lived under false pretences, and it got her down. She knew, for instance, what a gap there was between herself and the best professional actresses, but she couldn't prove it, because her mother kept her as the big light in a small amateur company. She had no job. She had no identity. Her mother lived a fantasy at her expense. She didn't love Alice. She loved her own image of Alice.

It did sound very much like Jennifer on Jennifer.

'Yes, of course it does, of course it does,' exclaimed Jennifer, as if I had spoken aloud. 'I'm in just the same position.'

'Mind you,' I said tentatively, 'that old lady told Rosalind a bit of something like this, and–'

'And Rosalind passed it on to us, yes. Believe you me, I am *not* getting my ideas from Rosalind.'

'I wish you weren't such enemies,' I said miserably.

'She's Clara's girl,' said Jennifer.

I went with a heavy heart into the shop. Rosalind was alone, dusting some Royal Doulton. I melted at the sight of her, stretching deliciously up to reach the shelf. So vulnerable, was Rosalind, under that lovely calm of hers.

She sensed that Jennifer had confided in me and I knew she expected to be told. I tried being jokey. 'The plot thickens,' I said, and put my arm round her. She did not respond.

'What does that mean?' She was cold, because I had been talking to Jennifer.

'Well . . . it's a long story. Tell you later.'

'Why not now?'

'Too many interruptions. This evening? We'll go to the Strolling Players again, shall we?'

'It's one way of spending an evening, I suppose.'

'I thought you wanted to collect evidence.'

'Do I?'

'Rosalind, is anything wrong?'

A mute shake of the head.

'You don't seem very cheerful.'

'I don't see why you can't tell me now.'

So I gave in and told her. I wasn't prepared for it and did it badly. Her face, as she listened, took on the guarded expression it had worn when we first met her. Her mouth set tight.

'No need to go to the Strolling Players, then.'

'Why not?'

'No point, if Jennifer can dream it all.'

'For Christ's sake, Rosalind. Why do you hate her so much?'

'I do not hate her. If I hated her, I'd hate you too. It's just that I'm made to feel an outsider. Can't you see that?'

A ridiculous argument now took place (twice interrupted by customers) as to who had had the closest contact with the ghosts. I said she had—Jennifer had only dreamed about them. She lumped Jennifer and me together, which gave Jennifer a big advantage. No, I said, I was the stooge for both of them. She took offence at this. Trying gamely to joke her out of it, I said I knew how a witch's cat must feel. This made things worse. Oh thanks, she said; when you didn't know a blind thing about your own parents it was nice to be told they were witches. I said nothing of the kind, I said. Then she was mistaken, she said, but I must excuse her, because, as I knew, she was very stupid, unlike some people.

It was all very childish, but before I could look round a serious quarrel was taking place. Then Rosalind said:

'Anyway, I don't know about that writing. I could have just done it myself.'

Now this, can you believe it, shook me more than anything that had happened before: more than the two apparitions, the hissing dolls, the lot. I felt as some very religious person might feel if his priest suddenly told him there was no God.

'But, Rosalind, you said—you said—'

'I know, but I made the squiggle with my own hand, didn't I?'

'But you swore you felt her guiding you—'

'I know, but maybe it's all in the mind.'

I felt betrayed. I had sudden awful misgivings. Rosalind might have imagined it all. Jennifer had dreamed it all. I alone had *seen* anything. Hallucinations?

I was so shattered that I actually forgot the phone ringing in the basement. That had been a shared experience and no delusion. But I forgot it. I lost my temper. I shouted:

'Can't believe a word you say, can I?'

Poor Rosalind went fiery red, and then looked so pale and piteous that I hated myself for hurting her so, but all the same I turned away from her, scowling like thunder. She always lost her nerve at such moments.

'Oh don't go like that. I'm sorry. Don't go.'

After a minute she said in my ear: 'Do we have to go on with it? Couldn't we just accept that this house is haunted and have done with it?'

'It's not the house, it's us.'

'It's messing us up,' she said dismally.

However, she went with me to the Strolling Players' place that evening, and became the usual efficient Rosalind, plodding through the photos and cuttings, and it did her credit, because 'research' was not her thing at all. In fact, she made our second find.

'Here's something.'

She pushed the cuttings book across the table.

OBITUARY
Miss Alice Crawley
Well-Known Amateur Actress

Miss Alice Crawley, second daughter of Mrs Violet Crawley, of 105 High Street, Mitten-on-the-Water, died last Monday, 25th May, after a short but intense bout of tuberculosis. The funeral took place at St Nicholas' Parish Church last Thursday. It was attended by her widowed mother and a number of friends from the Strolling Players Amateur Dramatic Society, of which Miss Crawley was an outstanding member.

She leaves a brother, at present serving with the army in India, and an elder sister, Clara, who was unfortunately prevented by illness from attending the funeral. A talented and versatile amateur actress, Miss Crawley . . .

Etc. I looked up.

'T.B.'

'Yes, not murder.'

'Clara didn't go to the funeral.'

'It says she was ill.'

'You told me once that people can will themselves to be ill. Did you learn that at college?'

'May have done.'

'Do you reckon Clara willed herself to be ill?'

'How do I know? Might have caught a cold.'

Something else occurred to me. 'You also said that people can even will themselves to die. Could they give themselves T.B.?'

Rosalind, normally the ministering angel, looked at me with a callousness that shocked me.

'Well, if she did, it lets Clara out, doesn't it?'

My father had lent me the car again – he really encouraged my going out with Rosalind – and so, having deposited her at the Rainham at the early official hour, I got home to find everyone still up. Every time I returned like this I weighed the chances of seeing a ghost again. I expected to meet one of them in the hallway, on the landing, on the stairs. Tonight in particular I should have been reassured to see both of them glide into the living-room and confront us all.

But our ghosts seemed to have to save up their strength to make an appearance, and we all went to bed that night without disturbance. I lay awake and thought. What Rosalind had said–'I could have done it myself'–kept repeating itself. She had begged me to believe that she hadn't really meant it, but the damage was done. If you could imagine yourself into illness, if imagination could even cause you to die, then I might well have imagined everything. And thus I worried myself into sleep.

When I woke again the house was in the deep hush of the small hours. And now the current between my sister and me was terrific. You know what it's like when you are on the phone and someone is listening in on the extension? I was 'live' to Jennifer, and if either of us had spoken, or even thought a speech, the other would have heard. But Jennifer was listening for another voice.

But no words came through, only a sort of hoarse straining from the throat, as if from someone gagged and terrified, unable to cry for help, fearing death perhaps; perhaps murder.

A young woman was making this sound. Alice.

It grew louder and more frantic till it became a groan. It lost tone and trailed off, harsh and hissing. Like the death rattle.

CHAPTER EIGHT

The next morning we did not say a word about it. We could hardly look each other in the eye. It was as though we shared something shameful, a secret of the night. It must have shown in our manner, because the tension at breakfast was almost unbearable. My father's face grew darker and darker. No word was possible. We ate in silence.

I thought and thought about it, of course, and I could feel Jennifer keeping pace with me. What we had heard suggested someone in mortal danger, or at least in mortal fear. It was dreadful, to have been summoned so urgently, and not to know what to do about it.

Then the doubts started by Rosalind began again. Jennifer and I were very close; could this all be some fantasy thing developed between us? She had scared me as a kid with her tales of Great-Aunt Clara on a broomstick at full moon, etc.; could it possibly be something that had grown out of that? Rosalind? Could I even have talked her into imagining things too?

Oh, no. This paperback psychiatry wouldn't do, you just couldn't make everything fit.

I passed Jennifer as she was going to do a stint in the shop.

'Oh, Jen,' I groaned, 'just when shall we work it all out?'

She smiled wanly. 'When it's full moon, maybe.'

Jennifer looked rotten. She was too low-spirited even to be irritable any more. My father fretted as if something inside him were eating him away. He kept soliciting her about her feelings, and was content to accept any snub in return. My mother said nothing, but watched her closely, rather like a referee on the point of stopping a fight. Even Rosalind, with her nurse's instincts, became quite motherly towards her.

'You see?' I said. 'She's concerned about you. She really likes you.'

'Nurses simply like patients.'

And then–just two weeks before the new term–a friend of hers named Debbie turned up with the offer of spending the rest of the holidays on her father's farm. Jennifer was in two minds about this. It was a lovely farm and Debbie was her best friend. On the other hand, absurd though it sounds, she was afraid that Rosalind and I might gang up with Clara while her back was turned.

My father was so anxious for her to go that he nearly stopped her doing so.

'But it's a grand opportunity, Jenny. You need to get some fresh air into your lungs.'

'There's enough of that in this draughty house without my filling my lungs with the stuff.'

'Ha ha! I like that! But seriously, darling, it would do you good.'

'I hate being done good.'

But she accepted, so as not to offend Debbie. When she said goodbye to me she became quite sentimental.

'This is a desertion.'

'I'll be all right. Go off and milk some cows.'

'Take care of yourself.'

She stood for a moment, slight and pert, but with eyes full of concern, and shadows under them. Then she actually kissed me, for the first time (if my memory serves me) in her life.

The day after Jennifer went away it was my parents' wedding anniversary. They went to the theatre in Gloucester, with a late dinner to follow. Rosalind and I, that same evening, went to see the Strolling Players, not to look through the records this time, but to see their show.

The Scout Hut rang and thudded. Rosalind was rapt and gleeful. She loved dancing. *The Boy Friend* was rather appropriate, because all the girls in it looked like Alice, but tonight we forgot Alice and her sister and their troubles. We forgot my sister too, and I think Rosalind felt that Jennifer for the time being had been not so much removed as exorcized.

The Rainham, for once, had given her a late pass, so she could get back any time within reason. My parents had the car, and so we had nowhere to go but back to my place, an attractive prospect, because finding anywhere to be alone with Rosalind was a continual problem. There was one obvious snag, though.

'You're not afraid of the ghosts?' I said, as we walked down the high street.

'*Yes*,' she said, and shivered and clung to me more closely. But we kept on heading for home, and somehow the atmosphere seemed wrong for ghosts tonight; too charged with echoes of the Charleston.

On leaving home, we had left our living-room light on to discourage burglars. It shone through the drawn curtains into the narrow side passage that led to our front door. When we entered this, we found it full of smoke.

I opened the front door and a billow of smoke poured over me. Rosalind sprang back, but I groped my way through the tiny hallway and into the living-room, shutting the door behind me. A lot of smoke had drifted in here, but the fire did not seem to have reached it. I dashed upstairs to my parents' bedroom, which was directly above the hallway and the living-room. The fire seemed to be confined to the one outside wall, and was not blazing but smouldering, although the window-frames and the sill were blackening and veined with red, and licked here and there by tiny tongues of flame. All this

I saw in the glimmer of light reflected from downstairs, because the lights had failed up here. I dragged whatever I could as far away from the window as possible and hurried downstairs again. Rosalind charged up the stairs, met me halfway, and dragged me spluttering and coughing into the street.

'Don't you go in again. Might fall in.'

'We must phone the—'

'I've done that.'

The fire engines arrived within a minute. From the firemen's point of view, this was a small fire, hardly having spread, by luck of the wind, to the inside of the house at all, and they put it out quite quickly, leaving a wake of sodden carpets and curtains and wallpapers, and water spurting sporadically out of cracks in miniature waterfalls. A small crowd had gathered, but decided it wasn't much of a show, and began drifting away. But to be fair, one or two neighbours gave us real support as we stood abjectly watching from the gutter. They brought us hot sweet tea and arranged to drive Rosalind home, as with my parents due to return at any time I really had to stand guard.

The fireman in charge made me sign a form and said, 'I've switched off your electricity. Tell your dad not to switch on again yet. I'm pretty well certain that faulty wiring started this fire.'

Rosalind shrugged wistfully at me and let herself be driven away. I declined another neighbour's offer of a bed for the night, found a torch, and then some candles, stuck them up in various spots and went round inspecting the damage.

I had saved the furniture in my parents' room from serious harm, but the carpet squelched underfoot and the window wall was a mess, and here was no place to spend a wedding anniversary night. Ours was a four-bedroomed house, and the spare room, untouched across the landing, had one single bed in it. I took Jennifer's bed to pieces and reassembled it in the

69

spare room. Then I carted from my parents' room all the things I thought they'd need and put them in the spare-room cupboard. All this I did in a hectic rush, obsessed with the wish to get everything done before they returned.

The spare room, the second best bedroom for size, had been Great-Aunt Clara's own room. She had kept it all her life. A cupboard, three feet deep, was let into the wall opposite the window and ran the whole length of it. At the far end of this cupboard was a miniature chest of drawers, much like the pieces we had in the shop, standing on a small work-table. We had as yet hardly entered this room since moving day. I had finished all I had to do by now and, for no particular purpose, I worked my way down to the little chest and opened the drawers.

There were four. The first two were empty. The third one contained a bundle of letters tied with dingy brownish ribbon.

I peered at the top envelope by the light of my torch. It was addressed to Miss C. Crawley and the stamp on it was an oldstyle three-halfpenny one. As I was trying to make out the date of the postmark I heard my parents come in downstairs. I put the letters back in their drawer, and then on impulse took them out again, slipped into my own room, and hid them under my pillow. Then downstairs to confront my thunder-struck parents.

Some neighbours had waited up for them and were already explaining the situation. They were making me a bit of a hero. I had dashed through smoke and flame to rescue our valuable stock. I hadn't, of course, but I let it stand.

'What a way to end a night out,' said my mother limply.

'Yes,' said my father. 'Thank God Jenny's away. This would have upset her badly.'

Then he remembered me, the other twin. 'Still, it might have been worse. The whole place might have burned down. You showed great presence of mind, John. I'm grateful to you.'

My mother hugged me suddenly. 'I should think your

evening was spoiled too, wasn't it, darling?'

'Yes,' said my father, and joined the group, with a hand on my shoulder. 'Jolly good, John. Rosalind all right, I hope?'

I told him Rosalind was all right. What I didn't tell him was that I had caused the fire myself. I'd realized this as soon as the fireman mentioned the wiring. On our first day in this house I had mended a fuse with a safety-pin. Safety-pins, unlike proper fuse wires, don't break under strain. I'd forgotten all about that.

During the next two days, while the insurance man, the builder, the plumber and the electrician nosed around the house, and nowhere was private, my problem was where to hide the bundle of letters. At last I stuffed them into an old school satchel and buried that under a pile of shoes in my wardrobe. I felt that they were visible through the door.

At the first opportunity I hid them under my pullover, walked with a stiff arm out of the house, and made for the reference library in the nearest town. There I chose the nearest corner and huddled over them, glancing furtively from side to side, as if expecting any moment a hand on my shoulder.

I hesitated. These *were* private letters. But surely, in view of how the late Miss C. Crawley was behaving, I had a right to any information I could get hold of? Or had I? I had not mentioned the letters to Rosalind yet, for fear she'd put me off. I sat before the bundle as if I were about to defuse a bomb. Well: I would just glance at them, to see whether they were relevant. I untied the ribbon.

It was brown only on the outside, where it had faded; underneath it was sky-blue. I looked through the envelopes. There were dozens of them, all in the same neat handwriting. I opened the top one.

> *'Dear Miss Crawley: I have to thank you, your mother and your sister for a really delightful evening . . .'*

71

He went on to say that he thought it absolutely 'ripping' of her to undertake making all those costumes for the next show. The inverted commas were his own; rather formal, he was. He said some things about rehearsals. He looked forward with very great pleasure to their next meeting. He was hers sincerely, Basil Hunter.

Basil, in the photo, with the patent leather hair. I was glad he'd enjoyed the cucumber sandwiches, anyway.

There were several more letters in this vein, in the course of which he began selling himself a bit. It seemed that he was a solicitor. *'My firm of Hansome, Hansome and Fellows . . . offering me a partnership . . . oldest legal business in Malvern . . .'* So. He was worth having.

The sixth or seventh letter began: *'My very dearest Clara: Wasn't last night heavenly? . . .'*

He had a fine literary style, Basil, and I guessed that he had rewritten his letters, to polish them, before sending them out. He seemed impressed with his own good luck. *'I hold you close to my heart, and all the while I marvel that you, so aloof in your loveliness, should be mine.'*

I thought of Great-Aunt Clara, that angular crone, and I marvelled too. Basil returned to the same point several times:

'I think of you, darling, as the Ice Queen whose heart my love has melted.'

Clara, it seemed, was no easy conquest. He was pretty sure of himself, though.

Rosalind was torn between eagerness to learn some good about Clara and dread that she might learn the worst. Her scruples worried her, too. But after a few 'Do you think we ought to?'s, she joined me in our sheltered corner in the café and read Basil's letters with me.

'Makes you wonder what her letters to him were like,' I said. 'Imagination boggles.'

'People talk quite differently to different people,' remarked

Rosalind. 'Like, you do yourself. You talk quite posh to me, but to your father you talk, like, uneducated.'

'Really?'

'Oh yers, reah-ly. What's "aloof"?'

'Up-stage. Hard to get at.'

'She was that all right. A real old dragon. But if she took to you she'd do anything for you. There was much more love in her than anyone knew.'

'She seems to have been the same all her life.'

'Well, with Alice being so cute and adorable I suppose she wanted to act the opposite. I wonder why she didn't marry this Basil?'

'Perhaps he never asked her.'

'Yes he did. Look at this—'

It was true; Basil not only wanted to marry Clara but seemed to be quite impatient about it. But the course of true love was meeting with some unusual frustrations.

> *'Why should your mother think that I have fallen in love with your sister? Darling, it really is most uncalled for and most embarrassing. Surely she cannot believe that because I have to pay court to Alice on the stage I am in love with her in earnest? Could you not, my dearest one, ever so discreetly explain matters to her? I would do so myself, but I cannot think of how to broach the matter, your mother is such a sensitive lady . . . '*

'I'll bet she was,' said Rosalind. 'She wanted a well-paid husband in tow so that her little darling could go on playing Columbine in comfort.'

'I wonder if Clara did try to explain?'

'Quite likely, but a woman like that wouldn't listen.'

'And just thought Clara was jealous?'

'Yes, right.'

'All the same, would any normal girl let that stop her?'

'Alice was taken ill.'

From the dates on the letters, Alice was taken seriously ill only a couple of months before she died. And now Basil's letters kept mentioning it.

> *'Of course I am deeply distressed, my darling—we of the Players all are—at your beloved sister's sad condition . . .'*
> *'I appreciate that your mother is quite distraught—I did indeed say that I loved Alice but not in that way—I am afraid she did not quite grasp what I meant . . .'*

'He was a very, very nice man, this one,' said Rosalind, reverently, 'and it's a great shame that she never married him.'

The letters, for all their stilted language, were becoming unbearably sad.

> *'We must accept, my dearest darling, that your dear sister's life is moving towards its close. Of course, of course I understand that you cannot consider our marrying while this grief hangs over you, but after the merciful release has come, be certain, my angel, that I shall be waiting for you, in the hope that my love and devotion will in some way assuage your grief . . .'*

'Well,' said Rosalind, dabbing at her eyes, 'what could be fairer than that?' She blew her nose gingerly; she had run out of tissues. 'And do you notice something? He keeps on about your *beloved* sister, your *dear* sister, your grief, and that, doesn't he? Doesn't look like Clara hated Alice that much, does it?'

'Well, Alice was dying.'

'I reckon she loved her. Ungrateful little twit.'

'But why didn't Clara marry Basil after Alice was dead?'

'Oh well, then her mother got ill, didn't she?'

'But according to Mum, she didn't last long, either.'

'No, right,' said Rosalind ruminatively. 'So she'd have been quite free to marry him then . . .' She shook her head slowly from side to side and said woefully, 'But she never did . . .'

We had been nursing tea for two for some two hours, and now the afternoon-tea customers were coming in, and the waitress was making meaning moves towards us.

'To be continued,' I said. 'Come on. Here's another tissue.

Make it last; it's all I've got left.'

Rosalind had dinner with us that evening. My father flirted with her, calling her 'the heavenly Rosa-lined', while she pretended to be amused. For reasons best known to themselves, they wanted to like each other, but they embarrassed me.

There were several letters still unread, and we rather dreaded reading them. Perhaps we should learn why Clara never married Basil? Perhaps he was scared off? Perhaps we should learn the nature of 'the dreadful thing' she had done, and perhaps Basil had fled from her as from a monster?

I felt quite agitated about it, but nothing like so much as Rosalind. I was amazed how emotional she got. It was as if Clara had been her own mother and she was facing some fearful family disgrace. She clung to me as we walked up the high street, looking up at me timidly.

'In any case, I've still got you.'

I felt touched and hugged her and tried to kiss her. It is difficult to do this walking along and we collided and stumbled. She stopped and embraced me as though it were to be her last act on earth. A beaky-nosed middle-aged woman, trailing a shopping bag on wheels, had to dodge round us, and gave us a look of sour disapproval as she passed.

We went to my old retreat, the reference library, which stayed open till eight o'clock this evening, and hid ourselves in a corner, passing the letters across the table to each other and conversing in whispers. The letters were both a relief and an anticlimax. No 'dreadful thing' was mentioned. Nothing specific was mentioned, except the illness of Clara's mother. Basil expressed sympathy for that, but, reading between the lines, you could tell that Clara's mother's illness was getting on his nerves. He had been writing for over a year now, and Clara, apparently, was still stalling him off. These last letters were notably short on love-talk. And then came the last letter of all. It was something of an ultimatum. He stressed the fact that he was now thirty-three and wanted to settle down with a wife and family. He mentioned his senior partner's daughter and said he was bound to confess he found her attractive. Although, of course, his devotion to Clara was unchanged . . .

So take him or leave him, Clara.

Nothing to do now but tie the ribbon round the letters again.

'He never had a chance,' said Rosalind.

'You mean Clara didn't love him back?'

'Oh yes, you can tell that from the way he writes to her. She couldn't have him because her sister wouldn't let her.'

Rosalind's face had taken on the same stony expression we had seen when we first met her. She gazed at me with great disappointed eyes.

'When Alice couldn't have everything she wanted, she got ill. When that didn't seem to be working, she died.'

'Oh, Rosalind, come on—'

'And then, just in case Clara thought she was free at last, Alice began haunting her. How could Clara marry with that happening to her?'

'What about the "dreadful thing"?'

'There's no proof she did anything at all.'

'This is all pretty fantastic.'

'You're the one who's seen her ghost, chum.'

'Well,' I said, still in a whisper, out of respect for the library, but a somewhat burning one, 'Clara and Basil couldn't get married. Bad luck. But they're not you and me. We're going to stick together whatever happens.'

Rosalind went pink with pleasure. 'Yes, we are. We are, aren't we?'

We walked slowly back to the Rainham, taking what you might call an extremely long short cut. I ought not to make snide remarks about our village and our district. It's a beautiful, peaceful part of the world, and we were lucky to live there and be in love there. I think Rosalind and I had never

76

been so happy as we were that evening.

We still talked of Clara and Basil, but a trifle smugly, almost as if pleased by the contrast between ourselves and them.

'You can understand how he felt,' said Rosalind. 'He couldn't wait for ever. Alice had her way.'

'You've got it in for Alice!'

'I reckon, if it hadn't been for Alice, it would have been perfect. Like, we'd be perfect if . . .'

Rosalind stopped.

'If . . . ?' I demanded.

'Nothing. Nothing, John. I didn't mean it. Oh please don't spoil it all . . . *please* . . . '

But I was not angry, and didn't feel like pretending to be. 'All right,' I said, 'I didn't say anything.'

'I've got you, haven't I?'

'I reckon you'd better eat me and make sure.'

'I love you, I do.'

It was that 'I do' that got me.

We had reached the great oak tree outside the Rainham grounds. 'Stop a minute,' I said.

'I really ought to go in . . . '

'Just a few minutes . . . '

And at that very moment, I felt the current; lightly at first, a slight trembling vibration; and then it was upon me in all its irresistible persistence. Jennifer was thirty or more miles away, but she might have been at my shoulder. I sensed a terrible anxiety, shot through with pleading. How can I put this in words? It was a 'don't condemn me, understand me' feeling. There was the sort of appeal in it that you see in the eyes of a dog. It was urgent like an S.O.S. I stood there, lost, for I don't know how many seconds.

'*John?*' said Rosalind.

I had taken her lightly by the upper arms, but I was standing in a daze. I had actually forgotten she was there.

I faltered, 'It's all right . . . it's just that . . . Jennifer . . . '

I did not know what I was saying. But Rosalind did. She turned away, sickened. She said in a low voice, 'Oh, *no!*'

She began striding away. I hurried after her.

'Rosalind, Rosalind, *please* . . . '

She stopped and turned briefly. 'No, John, it's not Rosalind please. I'm just not a match for the two of you. No, leave me alone.'

She hurried off out of my reach.

CHAPTER NINE

It was maddening, but there was no help for it. Perhaps Alice had waylaid Clara like this, and wrecked her chances with Basil. I wanted to chase after Rosalind, regardless of the consequences. But Jennifer's head was full of Alice and the knowledge of this was vibrating in my own. I felt helpless and desperate. Debbie's farm was thirty miles away, the hour was late, I couldn't borrow my father's car at such a time; and even if I could, what would Debbie's lot say if I turned up like a maniac asking for Jennifer?

I pictured my sister lying in the dark, possessed by that troubled spirit. There was no escape, and she had no-one to turn to. There was nothing I could do. Both girls were lost to me. I set off on the long drag home.

I was upset about Rosalind, I longed for Rosalind, yet not for two seconds could I concentrate on Rosalind. The current wouldn't allow it. It was like being on a bad telephone line. Two thirds of the way along my lonely journey another torment was added. Another force entered my mind. It tugged at me, as it were, like a fretful child at its mother's arm.

You've heard of split personality? I felt as if mine were in the actual process of splitting. The sisters, Alice and Clara—or rather, two forces of will emanating from them—were at war inside my head. I had been receiving Alice through Jennifer and now I was receiving Clara through Rosalind. Put baldly like that, it sounds mad. All right: I thought I was literally going mad. I felt my mind being pulled apart.

I reached the obelisk at the top of our deserted high street, and sat down, holding my head in my hands while the indescribable contest went on inside it. If the police had seen me at this moment, they'd have picked me up on suspicion of being on drugs. I even groaned aloud: 'Leave them alone, can't you? Stop setting my sister and Rosalind at each other. For God's sake leave them alone.'

Incredibly, this had an effect, like some instant answer to prayer. A sort of hush fell on my mind, as when a teacher walks into a classroom in uproar. I got up, sheepishly, and found that my shirt and pullover were drenched with sweat. I stumbled down the high street listening to the slapping of my heels on the pavement.

I must have been sitting by the obelisk for a long time, for when I got home my parents were in bed. I felt exhausted, yet to go to bed was out of the question. Perversely, I wanted to meet our ghosts, even though I knew they would chill me with fear. This, an actual wish for them, was something new and strange.

I crept into the shop, stared round in the light from the dress-shop, and then descended the wide stone steps to the basement. I always felt that the basement was the source of the haunting, even though strange things had happened elsewhere. I wondered why it should be. When Great-Aunt Clara had spoken of her sister 'below', had she meant this place? Or had she meant the grave underground?

The builder had taken down the damaged outside wall, and the room was shored up on huge jacks, or 'acros', as they were called. Canvas sheeting replaced the wall. The dolls and some other items had been moved to the centre of the room. They had suffered in the fire, most of them, and looked at me from agonized and drooping faces. I examined them and picked one or two of them up. They were nothing. I mean, they had no special significance: not 'witch's familiars' or anything of the kind, but simply objects with which Clara had been associated in life. She had some faint power over objects: a broomstick, a disused telephone, a sheet of notepaper–power, but not enough, so that what she wanted remained a mystery, as with a cat that keeps mewing and won't respond to offers of food.

So I did not speak to the dolls this time, but stood in the middle of the room, trembling and slightly sick, but calm, and spoke to my great-aunts in person. I was respectful, as if addressing them in prayer.

'Great-Aunt Alice. Great-Aunt Clara. Please tell me what you want us to know.'

I waited, as you would wait at the door of an empty house. Then, in a kind of nervous fidgeting, I checked the fuse-box to see that the proper wires had been put in. I moved a few things about in the room, needlessly, and then moved them back again. There had been no answer to my 'prayer'. Our ghosts didn't come when called. I went to the foot of the steps and switched off the lights. I stood for a moment and looked back into the room.

Chinks in the canvas sheeting let in a few gleams in the darkness. All along the opposite wall a line of old dressmaker's dummies was ranged, torsos on iron stands, padded out like pouter pigeons. There was a store of Victorian clothing in the shop and these dummies were used to show it off. Some of them were draped and some not. I found myself trying to pick out the draped ones. I could not stop looking at them. They had become of peculiar interest. Then, as though joining their ranks to stand in line with them, Clara and Alice appeared before my eyes.

They stood at least twenty feet apart, both were staring at me, and I was sure that they could not see each other nor were they aware of each other's presence. It was like the effect on a television screen where two speakers are shown in two different places. Alice was not in her Twenties get-up but in what looked like a nightgown, or the dress she had worn in the photo as Desdemona. She looked horrifyingly ill. She looked ghastly. I realized after a second or two that she was dressed in a shroud.

Clara was as we had last seen her in life: eighty-five, gaunt, and wearing a black dress hung about with strings of beads. The sheer ugliness of old age made her look evil, the picture of a witch.

Each was moving her mouth in speech, but no sound came. The effort to speak was intense and agonizing. With all my heart and soul I longed to hear their words. I was disappointed. No sound came. I don't know how long we stood like this. As they had arrived together, they faded together, and I was left staring into the line of dressmaker's dummies.

We assume that when people die they will join their departed loved ones in the world of spirit. These dead sisters had not joined each other. Each was alone and pleading from a void.

We had put up a 'business as usual' sign outside the shop, and the next morning Rosalind came in to work. As soon as I could, I crept in apprehensively with the object of making up to her. I did not have to wait long for this. The things in the shop had been shoved over to one side to allow access to the builders, and as soon as she saw me she drew me into a cubby-hole formed by a bookcase and a Welsh dresser and threw her arms round me.

'I've just got to understand you better, haven't I?'

Understand me! What girl wouldn't have been vexed with me last night?

'I'm sorry about last night,' I said. 'This sort of–don't know what to call it–telepathy thing between Jennifer and me is something we have to live with. It doesn't mean I don't love you. I do. That's what you've got to understand.'

I was rewarded with the rare smile. 'All right,' she said.

I pictured her lying awake all night, worrying. 'Did you

sleep all right last night?'

'Funny you should ask that. I had this dream. About Clara.'

'Did you? What time?'

'Couldn't say. Quite early on, I think. She was, like, on the other side of some sort of glass partition. I don't know where I was. Might have been in the shop. It was like she was trying to come in from the rain or something. She couldn't get in and she couldn't make herself heard. I knew she wanted to come in but couldn't do anything about it.'

'She never can get through, can she?'

'It was only a dream, though,' said Rosalind anxiously. 'See, we'd been talking about Clara all yesterday evening and she was on my mind—'

'Yes,' I said. I wasn't ready to tell her what had happened to me. Being reclaimed like this was almost worth the falling out, and I wanted to make the most of it. But I reflected that, as regards this 'telepathy thing', I was now getting it from both sides.

I went to a phone box and rang Jennifer at Debbie's farm. Our conversation would have puzzled a phone-tapper.

'Jen? It was Alice, was it?'

'Yes. Sorry I interrupted you, John.'

'Did she speak?'

'No. Just a feeling. Terrible anxiety. In the room with me, but she seemed to be on the other side of it and couldn't cross it to get to me . . . Frustration. Awful, awful frustration . . . '

'Jen? . . . Jen, are you there?'

'Yes, I'm here,' came her voice, faintly.

'Are you all right?'

'No, not really.'

'Farm no good?'

'The farm's great, but I can't hide in it. We're haunted, John. Wherever we go. Great for a girl who has to sleep with a nightlight, isn't it?'

'Jen, I'll keep in touch.'

'O.K. Or someone will.'

I went to my room, sat in my armchair, and put my feet up on my dressing-table.

Now, then.

When Clara was alive, she 'talked' to Alice–her sister 'below'–and perhaps saw her too.

But Alice, it seemed, couldn't talk back.

Now that they were both dead, they couldn't see or speak to each other. They wanted to but they couldn't. They had messages but couldn't deliver them. That row we heard in Jennifer's dream was not a quarrel, but two separate speeches overlaid, as each tried to make herself understood.

So? So each spirit had chosen a human being to work for her.

Clara had chosen Rosalind, because she had good reason to love Rosalind.

Alice had chosen Jennifer, because Jennifer seemed to be like her in temperament, and had the same sort of relationship with a parent.

Having plodded through the argument so far, my mind made a sudden jump. I saw now why Jennifer had told ghost stories as a little girl. They weren't just the inventions of an imaginative child. *Already, long before Jennifer could know what was happening to her, Alice's spirit was in touch with her.*

Although this hasn't taken long to write down, it took me a long, tortuous time to work out, and fairly exhausted me, and so far, I hadn't solved anything.

BUT, I went on:

I myself was the only one to have *seen* the ghosts.

I was the only one to be approached by *both* of them.

What was worst, they could approach, but they couldn't explain anything when they did. Any guesswork on our part was sure to be wrong.

I had clarified my thoughts, I suppose, but I was no wiser.

When would I be wiser?
Full moon?

While I was in this reverie, someone twice tapped on my bedroom door, and at last my mother came in and stood looking at me, with her head on one side.

'Penny for them! You were miles away!'

I took my feet from the dressing-table and sat up.

'Not quite yourself lately, John. Like a lost soul. It couldn't be reaction from that fire, could it?'

I shook my head. She sat on the edge of my bed. After a long silence she made one of her inspired statements.

'They're both very possessive, you know.'

I watched her very closely, and she went on: 'Rosalind is because you are her only human possession. That's why you must treat her so carefully.'

Then, after another pause, she said, almost as if to herself:

'Jenny doesn't like a stranger taking her brother away from her.'

Nothing profound in either of these statements, but they were loaded, all the same. She ought to have told fortunes. However, I replied bitterly:

'Dad does. He's overjoyed.'

'Not fair, John. He just can't win with you. If he were against Rosalind you'd call him a snob.'

I considered that I was always fair to my father, but I saw what she meant. She knew things without having to work them out. For the moment I had half a mind to tell her the whole story.

But I didn't. I could say that this was because I didn't want to worry her, but that wasn't the reason. She might cast doubt on my experiences, she might try to explain them away, and, God knew why, I dreaded that.

CHAPTER TEN

'Poor little thing,' said my mother, 'I found her reading the dictionary. She told me she wanted to improve her vocabulary.'

'She should learn it by heart,' said my father. 'If she could put it in order, she'd write a masterpiece.'

'I think it's very touching.'

'What's this in aid of?' I asked Rosalind later.

'I can read the dictionary if I want to.'

She would say no more, and grew sulky when I questioned her.

A day or two later Mrs Porter, at the old people's home, died.

'It was a mercy,' said Rosalind. 'It was degrading, living like that.'

A thought struck me. 'I wonder if Alice's death was a mercy? A mercy-*killing*? Overdose of drugs, something like that?'

'And that'd be the "dreadful thing" Clara did?'

'It gives, doesn't it?' I became excited. 'An act of pity. But we've seen from old Basil's letters what their mother was like–fixed ideas–madly unreasonable–can't you see her accusing Clara of murdering her sister? In order to have Basil, perhaps? And getting so uptight about it she actually went mad and died? Clara would have had Alice on her conscience–it's a big step to kill your own sister, even for mercy–and she'd have felt she'd killed her mother as well! Feeling like that, no wonder she never married Basil.'

'So why should Alice haunt Clara ever after?'

This stopped me. You couldn't believe that Alice simply wanted to express her thanks.

'So what's your explanation?' I said huffily.

'I reckon all Clara did was stay away from the funeral. Her mother made a terrific fuss and it, like, exaggerated itself in Mrs Porter's mind.'

'And Alice haunted Clara for *that?*'

'Can't say, can you?' said Rosalind, vexed.

We both sulked for a while.

'Mrs Porter is being cremated,' said Rosalind at last, as though proffering a consolation. 'The undertaker has taken the body to a chapel of rest.'

'Oh, yes?'

'Alice was buried, though. In those days they kept the coffin in the house till the day of the funeral. Where do you think they kept hers?'

The stairs to the upper room were narrow and twisty. In the living-rooms you'd be seeing the thing all the time. There was only one place, easy of access and discreetly out of the way.

'In the basement.'

We eyed each other.

Jennifer and her friend Debbie were opposites. Debbie was rosy and horse-crazy, while Jennifer liked country life best on ornamental plates. As opposites often do, they got on fine. Jennifer loved the farm. So why did I feel as if in the first stages of a cold?

Well, the current was active. It was faint and weak, and carried no news, but it persuaded me that Jennifer was not as happy as she ought to be. She would pretend to her friends to be bubbling with joy, of course. She was good at that. But she couldn't pretend with me.

Rosalind knew how I felt. She watched me so closely that I expected her any minute to take my temperature. She was determined to 'understand' me, as she had said, but she was not finding it easy. I could reason myself hoarse; Jennifer was not a rival but my sister; the current was just a wave-length and had nothing to do with love. Rosalind would nod agreement. Yes of course she understood. Then she would say:

'But you do put her first, though, don't you?'

'I've told you–'

She understood in her head, but not in her heart and guts.

I kept thinking of the phrase 'full moon'. It had a private meaning for Jennifer and me. 'When it's full moon' meant 'when the ship comes in', 'when the cows come home',–something like that. I thought of our present state as like the moon in quarters, or crescents, with Alice in one quarter holding Jennifer hostage, and Clara in another doing the same with Rosalind. They were in rival territories, like enemy countries separated by the sea and joined by the land underneath. Those rival territories, those quarters, needed to be brought together to make the full moon, and then everything would be explained. If Rosalind and Jennifer could only unite, then our cold and grieving ghosts could come together too, and whatever was to be forgiven would be forgiven. But 'if only' always means that the case is hopeless.

My 'cold' grew worse. I was sure that Jennifer was ill, getting lower and lower on that healthy farm as the spirit of Alice worked on her. Rosalind had said that Alice got her own way even if it meant dying for it. Now Alice had no life to lose. I feared for my sister. I wanted to get between her and Alice as I had done so far. I was afraid that if I waited too long she would succumb completely, and that when we were finally called to her bedside we should find not Jennifer but Alice lying in her place.

No, that is not quite true. I didn't really believe it; it was a fantastic fear; and I was taken aback when Debbie's folk rang up to say that Jennifer had really been taken ill.

She had fainted in the kitchen just after breakfast. She had a temperature and they had put her to bed. The doctor had called and vaguely diagnosed nervous exhaustion. Yes, better take her home.

The words 'nervous exhaustion' appalled my father. He looked as if he were suffering from it himself. He was rather given to putting on an act, as he did at the funeral, but there was no doubt he was genuine this time, and he blamed himself bitterly. 'This is my doing. I've not overworked her, but I've pestered her. I've never let her alone.'

My mother pursed her lips. She was not her usual unruffled self. 'You really must *not* blame yourself for everything,' she said, reproving him rather than comforting.

'Drive us there, John?' said my father.

'Sure.'

He cleared his throat and said, apparently with difficulty: 'I know you're worried for her. I know you're very fond of her.'

He'd never said such a thing before in his life.

I drove our new Maestro out into the country and up the lurching quarter-mile track to the farm. Fergus, the dog, leapt ecstatically all round us when we got out in the yard, but Debbie came out with an anxious look so unnatural to her that it might have got on to the wrong face by mistake, and both her parents followed, looking solemn and slightly guilty. They were always protective to Jennifer, believing her to be excessively delicate, with her habit of eating one slice of toast for breakfast instead of the massive fry-ups they were used to, and they spoke to us rather ashamedly, as if their own coarseness had caused her illness. They had tried to make her eat a cooked breakfast, they said, because they thought she looked peaky and needed building up, but after dabbing at it she had apologized, pushed it away, and started to go to her room, but had collapsed in the doorway, whereupon Debbie's father had carried her upstairs and the whole family had hovered about her ever since, giving her every attention short of the kiss of life. We followed Debbie up to the large, timbered, low-ceilinged bedroom. Jennifer was dressed to go back with us and was sitting in an armchair by the radiator. She gave us a wan, apologetic smile. When we spoke to her she turned away, as if the mere sound of our voices were bringing on tears.

Seeing her dispersed the fantasies I had been building up while driving here. I had half expected to see Alice's face superimposed on hers, like two photographs on one print. Nothing like that. But it was the shell of herself that I saw.

Almost, you might say, the ghost of herself.

I drove slowly and smoothly home and my mother helped Jennifer to her room. Rosalind was serving in the shop. Without speaking, she motioned to me to take her place, and became the nurse-elect, following my mother and remaining with her until Jennifer was put to bed again. As soon as it was seemly for him to do so my father went in and sat by her.

The doctor at the farm had given Jennifer a prescription, and Rosalind now took this to the chemist's. When she came back she talked quietly to my mother on the landing for a while. Then she joined me in the shop, where I was feeling like a discarded spare part.

I began to say something superfluous like 'She's all in, isn't she?' but stopped when I saw Rosalind's face.

'Families,' she muttered.

Then: 'It's all happening again, isn't it?'

I knew what she meant, but I gave her so hard a look that she lost her nerve.

'I didn't mean it! John! I didn't mean it!'

Oh, I was so torn between the two of them. I hated her for putting the boot in while Jennifer lay up there so ill, yet I knew just what she meant and how she felt, and I loved her for being so passionately concerned. I felt that she was just as ill as Jennifer, in her own way, and I took her hands and tried to comfort her.

'I know just what you mean, and I do understand, but look, you're a nurse, be practical, don't make a mystery of it. She'll be all right and so will we.'

But instead of calming down she began to talk wildly. 'Clara has dropped out. She can't get to us any more. She's not strong enough. She never was a match for Alice. *Alice is winning, can't you see?*'

I became angry again. 'Winning *what?*'

She put her hands to her face and sobbed.

We did not go out that evening, but watched television, although goodness knows what it was we watched. My father was turning the stairs into a treadmill. He offered to lend us the car. When I refused he said:

'No, I understand, John. You want to stay home. You feel like a doctor on call.'

Before I could ask what he meant by this he went on: 'Oh, I know there's an uncanny link between you and Jenny. Telepathy, would you call it? I am afraid I've been rather crass about it in the past. Sheer selfishness on my part.'

Of course, he would never speak plainly if he could help it, but all the same, this was an amazing concession on his part. Never before had I heard him admit that I was fit for anything, except to fit a new washer on a tap or pump up the tyres of the car. Still, I thought, don't be too delighted. It was only for Jennifer's sake he was saying this. He was turning to me as a last resort, rather as people turn to a faith-healer when an ordinary doctor can't cure them.

I drove Rosalind home and we lingered for a while under the oak tree. Usually it was I who tried to delay these partings, but this time she clung and clung to me so long that I became impatient to get away.

As I was going to bed my father said to me, in tones almost sepulchral, 'If she calls you, go to her, John. You may be her salvation.'

It was his nature to dramatize things, and you would have thought, to hear him, that he was waiting for the onset of doom itself. I wondered, did I dramatize too? I was his son; was I running off his batteries, so to speak? Anyway, it was sad to see someone so self-assured and witty in such a state, pleading for help; and Jennifer was wrong, he did not see her just as a prize-winning projection of himself; he really loved her. It softened me towards him, and there was more affection between us than there had ever been before.

As for 'if she calls you', he simply did not understand our affinity; Jennifer didn't call me, the current was there all the time, dormant or active, and when it grew strong I was drawn to her by some magnet beyond my control. But I gave him my promise and looked in on Jennifer to say goodnight. She lay open-eyed and slack in a trance of blank wakefulness. Only her light brown eyes moved to meet mine, and for the fraction of a second I saw in them a glint of red.

'Talk to me,' I said. But terror was caged up behind her eyes, and she would not or could not answer.

In spite of everything, I slept until about three in the morning. Midnight is supposed to be the 'witching hour', but the small hours really are so, when your vitality is low. When I awoke I knew that she was delirious. She was making no noise, but her mind was a kaleidoscope of wildly shifting scenes, and the extraordinary thing was, it was throwing up pictures of people she had never seen in life. She had never seen Rosalind's album nor any of the evidence at the Strolling Players' place, but now they loomed up and reeled and faded. Alice in various costumes, Basil, Clara, young as she was in the photo and old as she had been at her death, and a riot of other faces and places. They came and went too fast to be grasped, in sickening confusion.

I strove with all my being to concentrate, to hold them still, to make them obey me. And then, against my will, as if I were

92

drugged, I drifted into sleep. I myself began to dream; or rather, I entered Jennifer's dream; I took it over from her, and left her in peace.

CHAPTER ELEVEN

I called her in my head, softly and experimentally: 'Jen? Jen?' and was relieved when she did not answer.

I found myself on the landing. The dolls were back, fresh and new, in glass cases which I had not seen before. The whole house looked different. There was another carpet on the stairs. I went downstairs, through our living-room, and into the shop; but no, there was no shop, no glass door, just an ordinary room with bay windows, over which venetian blinds were drawn.

By the window there was a Victorian horsehair sofa. I moved close enough to touch it when I saw that there was a woman lying on it. She wore an embroidered housecoat, underneath which I saw the hem of a nightdress, and bedroom slippers on her feet. She was strikingly like both her daughters, and had once been beautiful, but her face was lost and wretched.

I was looking on at all this, as you would at things on a screen. Even so, when she rose to walk across the room, I instinctively made way for her. She went through the back room, up the stairs, and into 'Jennifer's room', which of course was not to be Jennifer's room for many years to come. I was reluctant to follow her, but waited on the landing, by the dolls. A low wail came from the room, then a continuous, half-crazed moaning. She came out, her hands plunged into her long hair, which fell wildly about her face. She took two uncertain steps, leaned against the wall, and became rigid. She moaned ceaselessly: 'Alice . . . Alice . . . Alice . . . '

I lost touch with this. I was no longer on the landing, and the woman had gone. I found that I was in the basement. A long table in the centre supported a coffin with its lid open. I went up to it and saw that it contained Alice, with her hands folded on her breast. Her cute face had wasted away to the very shape of the skull, and her eyes stood out like marbles under their closed lids.

Clara came down the steps. It was the young Clara, the one Rosalind and I had seen in the photo. She wore a long quilted dressing-gown. Her hair was loose about her shoulders.

She stopped and waited at the foot of the steps. The muscles of her face worked and worked. Her eyes were burning.

She came right up to me beside the coffin, and stood there for a long time. Her face was mere inches from mine, and it froze me to the bone to see it hardening. From inside her dressing-gown she drew a long knife, a kitchen knife, sharpened to a slender wand of steel.

The other woman, the mother, appeared on the steps. She let out such a scream of horror that you would have thought it had strength enough to kill. Clara tensed up as though stabbed through with mortal pain. The knife clattered from her hand. The mother stumbled across the room, her eyes rolling in her head. She fell down at Clara's feet with her mouth gaping open. Where her face dragged on the floor I saw a line of dust form on the edge of her tongue.

And now everything ran riot in a flickering, bewildering succession of images without connection, and I was awake in my own world, in my own bed.

My father went into Jennifer's room the next morning, reverently bearing a cup of tea.

She sat up, stared, yawned, and stretched.

'I'm hungry!' she said.

I had drawn out her dream like poison from a wound, and she was well.

95

My father half guessed what had happened. He was delighted and excited and puzzled. When I came down to breakfast he gave me a mystic smile.

'Behold, the dreamer cometh!'

And then he kept asking questions. We couldn't explain, and still less could he understand. His trouble was, he had to be an authority on everything that interested him, and build his own theory round it, and so the bare truth was hard for him to grasp.

'What strange pair have I sired?' he enquired of the air.

And then, like the teacher he was, he explained everything to us. Jennifer was ultra-sensitive, and so imaginative that her body could not always stand up to the force of her mind. Her brain created visions that mine was too dull to comprehend, but she was too delicate to control them, and so she passed them on to me, her general handyman. I bore the brunt of her sensibilities.

'Yes, Dad,' I said. 'It's a good arrangement, isn't it?'

'It's a fascinating psychological phenomenon,' he said severely. To be fair, he'd got it more or less right, except that Jennifer didn't *imagine* anything. Her mind picked up the feel of things. It picked up truths.

Unfortunately, it hadn't picked up the whole truth. Either she was too sensitive to stand any more, or else Alice, perhaps, had found it unbearable to go on and broken down. She'd left us a cliff-hanger, I must say.

What had Clara been going to do? She'd left it too late for murder, hadn't she? I turned over all kinds of possibilities, until they became too gruesome to bear thinking about.

I bullied Jennifer about it.

'You keep saying you know just how Alice felt, so why can't you explain this?'

'I know how she *felt*, but not what *happened*. Can't you understand the difference? I only know she was terrified. And guilty.'

'She should be the last one to feel guilty.'

'She hated her mother.'

'And her sister too, I should think.'

'No, her mother.'

'Her sister certainly hated her.'

'I'm not sure,' said Jennifer, distressed.

'Surely—'

She held her temples. 'Don't keep on at me. You ought to know, not me. You're supposed to be the clearing-house for my hang-ups, aren't you? All I could feel was . . . oh, I don't know. Terrible confusion, as if everyone had got the wrong idea and Alice was hysterically trying to put them right. Because they wouldn't *listen* . . .'

'Who are *they*?'

'I don't know. Leave me alone. I felt all right till you started.'

'All right, Jen,' I said hastily, seeing the danger signs.

'You're like a bull at a gate. You be careful how you tell that poor kid about it.'

'That's funny, coming from you.'

'She's got more feeling than any of us.' Then, cross with herself for showing such softness, Jennifer added: 'She should mind her own business, though. Why should she get so uptight about some old woman she met by accident? She must meet dozens of them, do-gooding round the old folks' home.'

'I shan't tell Rosalind.'

'I bet you do.'

Yes; in deciding that, I had reckoned without Rosalind.

'Jennifer's recovered quickly.'

'Yes, hasn't she.'

'That's good, then.'

'Yes, we're all glad.'

Rosalind drew me behind the Welsh dresser and gave me that frank stare that was her strongest weapon.

'Tell me.'

I gave in. 'All right . . . not here, though. It's too . . . there's too much. I'll tell you later.'

'Just say – is it bad?'

'Afraid so.'

'Ask a silly question,' said Rosalind disconsolately.

To our indignation, our favourite spot in the café was occupied by two wretched intruders, and we had to go to the cafeteria in Woolworth's and huddle in a corner amid the clatter of cutlery, which did, however, provide a cover for our conversation.

Rosalind listened, looking defiant and miserable.

'You can't believe in dreams, though. Not literally. They, like, symbolize things, don't they?'

'Not this. I think it really happened.'

'John, this is like that party game where you whisper something round a circle and it ends up completely altered. You got a dream from Jennifer and she got it from Alice, and who's to say Alice wasn't all mixed up or just plain telling lies?'

Mixed up: yes, Jennifer had said something like that, too. But as I was trying to recall it, Rosalind swept on:

'Look, Alice has been dead for ages. We didn't know her, we've no idea what she was really like, whatever Jennifer says about *feelings* and that. I *did* know Clara, I knew her better than any of you, and I tell you, she was not cruel or wicked or anything like it, she was proper soft inside, so soft that she had to act tough, to, like, protect herself. She couldn't possibly have –'

'But you knew her as an old woman.'

'She was always the same. Didn't Basil say she was an Ice-Queen and aloof and that? And didn't he say she loved her sister? Didn't he go on about her beloved sister and her grief and that?'

'She may have been –'

'Putting on an act for him, like? Oh, no. You don't understand women. Girls always moan about their families to

98

their boy-friends. They like to seem like little Cinderellas, they do. But Basil was sure she loved her.'

'You ought to be a defending counsel, not a nurse.'

'She needs defending. I reckon she missed out all along the line. Alice was everyone's pet and she was the nasty sister. Then Alice dies and that spoils things for her with Basil. Then all the neighbours take against her and call her a witch. Then she dies, but she's still the villain, because Alice starts Jennifer dreaming and you're there to back her up and – what are you smiling at?'

'Anyone who overheard this would think we were mad.'

'Most families are mad, if you look into them.'

'Clara's got you, anyway.'

'She can't get through to me.'

Then Rosalind gave me a look that alarmed me.

'I wonder if I could get through to her?'

'Don't you go looking for trouble! It's one thing looking up old theatre programmes, but don't you try getting in touch with spirits. It's not a thing to meddle with.'

'Hark who's talking!'

'We've never tried to call them up. They've come to us.'

'Clara's come to me as well.'

'That's all right, then, isn't it?'

'No, she needs help. She's always needed my help.'

'She's dangerous, Rosalind.'

'I was never afraid of her when she was alive and I'm not now.'

Without bothering to ask what Rosalind intended to do I said angrily, 'You just leave well alone!'

She flushed and stared down into her teacup. I looked at the glossy crown of her head and was about to apologize when she looked up and said sulkily:

'I'm not going to do nothing.'

I took this at the time to be simply bad grammar. I was to find that I was wrong.

CHAPTER TWELVE

For the next few days everyone was in better spirits. My mother went back to work–the junior schools started earlier than ours–and for the last week-end of our holidays Debbie came to stay with us, and Jennifer went swimming with her, and played tennis with her, and was 'taken out of herself', as the saying goes. Our ghosts were dormant, as if they too were recuperating from that recent drama.

The basement was now rebuilt, and opened to the public. This let in fresh air and took the spookiness out of it, and in this new climate I was off-guard, and even doubtful about what I thought I had seen. I'm a very uncertain person. I can be talked out of anything by anyone, especially myself.

Rosalind, too, was cheerful–a bit too cheerful, now that I look back on it: slightly artificial, rather as she was when she spoke to Jennifer. It suited me, though; I'd had enough of gloom for a while. She had a flair for window-dressing, and she busied herself in the basement, posing the junk to look saleable, and continually changing it around, as if she were arranging flowers.

Some of the dolls had been damaged by the fire, and needed new clothes and new parts. Rosalind paid the most loving attention to them, sorting them out in order of injury, parcelling them up for the 'dolls' hospital', and occasionally cradling them in her arms.

'Child-substitutes,' said my father.

'Possibly, but she's really short of parents, not children,'

100

said my mother.

Rosalind and the dolls! I should have been more awake.

I had an uneasy night. It was not the current. Jennifer, for once, was happy, because Debbie was staying with us, and I could sense this without needing to dwell on it. But I myself felt a vague unease, as if another current were trying to come into existence and couldn't tune in. I kept thinking of Rosalind, and whenever I pictured her in my mind I saw Clara as well. Their phantoms loomed and faded, and I grew more and more restless until I was really keyed-up. I fostered wild schemes of ringing Rosalind or even calling on her, but of course I made no attempt to carry them out.

The next morning she, like us, was to go back to college, but she was to have the afternoon free, and promised to work in the shop. But at lunch-time Claire Waltham rang my mother at school. Please excuse Rosalind. No, nothing serious. But strange. 'Look,' said Claire Waltham, 'I think I'd better pop round. About a quarter to four?'

'Yes, of course,' said my mother, and spent the rest of the day making troubled conjectures, most of them concerning me.

By five o'clock, when the rest of us got home, Mrs Waltham had told her tale. The night before, she had gone on her usual round before turning in–this would be near midnight, as she kept late hours. The Rainham was a well-appointed place. Every girl over fourteen had a room of her own, and even the seven-year-olds shared rooms with not more than four others. It was from one of these cells of seven-year-olds that Mrs Waltham heard giggling. She opened the door a crack. 'Settle down,' she said. Then: 'I *said:* settle *down!*'

Silence. But she had only gone a few steps when it started again. She turned back, cross, when she heard similar noises from another room. She listened, and now she realized that every room in the corridor was in a state of giggles, beyond control, laced with tears.

She went up a floor and listened again. In this corridor the girls shared in pairs. There were twelve rooms. She listened briefly at each one. Spluttered laughter, muffled sobbing, an occasional wail.

Mrs Waltham was a woman of steady nerves, but she was shaken, partly because she was unsure how to deal with this, and partly for an indefinable reason, an atmosphere that had got into the place and was turning her cold. She went upstairs again, to the floor where the seniors enjoyed their private rooms. Sounds of suppressed weeping came from every one of them, with one exception. Rosalind's.

This, in contrast, was like the tomb. She stood outside, and was dismayed to discover how much she was trembling. The girls' hysteria rose up round her, not loud, but intense, a mass jitters.

Nervous crises were not uncommon at the Rainham. There was a tremendous corporate spirit in the place, and any emotional disturbance could start a chain reaction. It happened sometimes when a lost parent turned up to claim one of the girls. But there had never been anything before on this scale, and Mrs Waltham wondered if something really nasty had happened–had one of the girls been assaulted and come home in distress?–something like that? No, she would have surely heard about it, nor would it have such an effect; the Rainham would be ablaze with indignation, not awash with tears.

Miss Pearson, one of her staff, came on to the landing, wearing a dressing-gown and a startled look.

'Whatever's–?'

'I don't know, Margaret. Seems like an epidemic.'

'Is Rosalind–?'

'Seems the only sane one left.'

There was no head girl at the Rainham, but Rosalind was the uncrowned one, as it were.

'She might help,' said Miss Pearson. 'They all dote on her.'

Mrs Waltham nodded. They went into Rosalind's room.

Her bedside lamp was on. She was kneeling on the floor with her back to it, her hands clasped tightly together, her eyes wide and staring. One of our dolls, an Edwardian one with a half-melted face, was propped up on the bed beside her.

Mrs Waltham managed to sound casual. 'Yoga meditation, Ros?' she asked mildly, while shivers ran through her. 'Sorry to interrupt, but we have a sort of trauma out here–'

Rosalind neither saw nor heard her. Mrs Waltham knelt down and took her hands.

'Rosalind. Wake up.'

Rosalind looked at her with far-away eyes. She said, not in her own voice, but in an aged croak:

'Make sure that I am dead.'

Mrs Waltham went white, but she still managed to sound off-hand and friendly. 'If I'm ever in doubt, I certainly will. Wake up, dear.'

Rosalind came to and looked guilty.

'I'm sorry–'

'No need. Dreaming, were you?'

'That's right. I was dreaming.'

'You were talking in your sleep,' said Miss Pearson accusingly.

'Oh! What was I saying?'

'Nothing,' said Mrs Waltham, cutting in quickly. 'We came to ask you to help. The girls seem rather disturbed.'

Together they looked into every room in turn, but the fever, or whatever it had been, had subsided. The girls were bewildered, or cross, or simply asleep.

'Wonderful,' said Mrs Waltham. 'The Lady with a Lamp.'

'What was the matter?'

'It's all right now. Tell you tomorrow. You must get some sleep. So must we.'

'Phew!' she said, when Rosalind had gone.

'I thought at first she might be on drugs,' said Miss Pearson. 'I thought they all might have been experimenting.'

'No. She was having a nightmare.'

'But the girls–'

'Yes, girls are mysterious things. There are some heavy crushes on Rosalind here, and I can only suppose it was some sort of psychological infection. Extraordinary. Do let's get to bed, shall we?'

'Are you all right?'

'Perfectly, thanks.'

Then Mrs Waltham fainted.

I think that children and young people must have some kind of sixth sense that they lose in middle age. My mother and Mrs Waltham were understanding ladies, but they didn't get near to the real cause of the Rainham disturbance. They mentioned witchcraft. They agreed that Great-Aunt Clara might have dabbled in it, and might have passed on a few tricks to Rosalind, and that Rosalind might have been trying one out with the doll. But they explained it all away by psychology. They agreed that Rosalind had been devoted to Clara, the substitute aunt, and doted on us, the substitute family, and that her strong feelings had communicated themselves to the girls, who had crushes on her. My father took this up and revelled in it. He told us a story of some convent where all the nuns were supposed to be possessed by devils and went raving mad. Mass suggestion, he assured us. My mother put in a bit about rivalry between Rosalind and Jennifer, and my father lectured on our 'affinity', as if he'd invented it. There was truth in all this, but not the whole truth. No-one dreamed what had really happened: that Clara's spirit had been summoned by Rosalind and had ranged the orphanage straining to get through to her. No-one saw that Rosalind's experience had nothing to do with either witchcraft or psychology. No-one saw that 'mass suggestion', however scientific it sounds, is as far-fetched as any other notion. Mrs Waltham, who had been thoroughly scared, clung to it in relief.

'I am ashamed to admit,' she said, 'that I even toyed with the idea of calling the Vicar out to exorcize evil spirits! The power of suggestion! You don't realize it till you experience it!'

They agreed that the best thing was to leave Rosalind alone, not to question her.

'Now: what's your version?' said Jennifer to me, later.

'Clara got a stage further than she did on the phone. It was her voice they heard, not Rosalind's.'

'But what did she mean? "Make sure I'm dead"? The crematorium did that.'

I visited Rosalind at the Rainham that evening, carrying a bunch of flowers, like coals to Newcastle, because there were vases of them on every shelf and in every corner. I expected the girls in general to look a bit sheepish about the previous night's weep-in, but not a bit of it. They gave me the usual curious glances, that was all. Weep-in taken for granted and forgotten. I shall never understand girls.

Mrs Waltham waylaid me: 'John. Don't tell her what she said in her sleep, will you?'

'No, all right.'

'It might upset her. Just nonsense, anyway.'

She was good at making light of things, Mrs Waltham, and I hoped she'd go on doing so. I didn't want her, or any other older person, getting involved.

I was allowed to see Rosalind in the Interview Room, in private.

'What have you been up to?' I said.

'Getting nowhere.'

Rather shamefacedly, she explained. She had decided that all our supernatural evidence was coming through Jennifer, and on to me, from Alice. She wanted Clara's version. But she was (as she so often insisted) an outsider. She couldn't dream dreams and have visions. And then it occurred to her that Clara had always tried to communicate through objects: the broom, the dolls, the telephone, the writing pad. Now, Mrs Porter had said, 'She did so love her dolls!', and moreover, the dolls were being posted away for repairs and it would be easy to borrow one, and so—

'I was going to give it back, though,' said Rosalind.

'Yes, sure. Go on.'

Well, having decided on this one-person séance, she was uncertain what to do. She put the doll on her bed, propped up against a pillow, and sat in front of it with her writing pad in her hand, feeling rather silly. She 'concentrated'. She kept staring at the doll, repeating again and again, 'Miss Crawley? Are you there? If you are, speak to me . . .' She kept at it until three dolls swam in front of her and she got pins and needles in her legs.

And then, after as long as two hours of this, the spirit responded, and she felt its presence, like gathering darkness, like awareness of cold. She was frightened, not for herself, but for what she might learn. Like all natural nurses, Rosalind was tough, and could have watched a hideous operation without flinching, where anyone normal would have passed out, and when she had said that she wasn't afraid of Clara alive or dead, she was telling the simple truth. But now she felt that some terrible thing was about to be told, and although she was asking it, she did not want to know. She felt as you would if you got a letter you dreaded opening. Her resolution wavered.

She broke off.

'I always thought the most wonderful thing in the world was to have a family, to belong to someone. Don't think I'm like one of those deprived girls you see in these social dramas on the telly, because I'm not, the Rainham's very good, quite a showcase, but once you're there, everyone thinks, well, that's fine, and no-one will ever try to get you out. Do you know what every Rainham girl dreams about? Being adopted. By some marvellous rich adoring foster parents. And loved. Because at the Rainham you're cared for and that, but not loved.'

'I love you.'

'No, you desire me.'

I looked at her in wonder, she sounded so wise and old-fashioned, but she went on: 'Well, Clara, like, adopted me. And I adopted her. I loved her. I prided myself that I was the one who understood her, she was mine. I wanted to go on loving her. I still want to love her. If she did some awful thing I don't want to know about it. She shouldn't have let me think she was good. She shouldn't have let me love her . . .'

And so the gathering strength of Clara found itself up against the barrier of Rosalind's resistance. The tension this created was so great that she expected some physical outcome of it, like lightning. The doll began to shimmer and glow with light. She had put her small table-light on, whose light could hardly be seen under her door, and placed the doll in front of it. To look at the doll became unbearable. She moved it so that she could turn her back to her lamp, and cast her own shadow on the doll, but when she had done so, the doll was still haloed with white light. It held her gaze. Its damaged little face was alive with purpose. Its beady eyes glittered.

'She was really close then,' said Rosalind. 'She was in the room.'

'Did you see her?'

'No. I've never seen her, only in a dream. Like Jennifer. I think that was what she was trying to make me do ... dream ...'

'Did you dream?'

'Not that I remember, but I do know she said something to me in my sleep.'

I feared what might come next, but to my relief she didn't ask any questions. For several moments she was lost in her own thoughts.

107

'She wanted to die, she did.'

'Well, I suppose at her age–'

'No, that's not what I mean. I can see it now. All her talk about being at peace, and that. She didn't mean herself, she meant Alice. She wanted to die so that she could meet Alice in her own world and then everything would be all right. Like, forgiven and that. But it hasn't worked out. You do something wrong, don't expect to get away with it.'

She spoke with such despair that I longed to console her, with lies if necessary.

'Jennifer and I may have got it wrong–you said yourself–you know–Alice's version–'

'You don't believe that.' And she repeated: 'You do something wrong, you have to pay for it. Like my mother, whoever she was. I reckon she's paid for it all right.'

She was wrong, I really did love her, and I'd have done anything to comfort her, but I could think of nothing.

'Anyone would say, I'm much better off in the Rainham than living with a slag like that. But you see what happens? I find me one of these substitute mothers, and what do I get?'

CHAPTER THIRTEEN

What worried me most about Mrs Waltham's tale was what she said about calling in the vicar. Sooner or later, I thought, *someone* will be called in–a psychiatrist or some such. We wouldn't be able to keep the thing to ourselves. Yet we must. Once outsiders started dissecting us, we'd never piece the full moon together.

I was sorry my mother had heard the story. She would guess things, and ask questions. She would question me, not the girls.

Jennifer had a grudge against her. 'She never takes me seriously, that woman. She patronizes me. She pats me on the head like a dog.' This opened my eyes. I had thought Jennifer everybody's darling, but I saw what she meant. There was always the faintest hint of amusement in my mother's attitude to Jennifer, as if she thought too much fuss was made of her.

As for Rosalind, my mother behaved to her as you would to a patient in hospital. She saw the pathetic orphan in everything she did. She'd never question her for fear of hurting her feelings.

She had told me, 'They draw their strength from you.' I'd never known what she meant by this, but in ways she couldn't know, she was right. 'They' included everyone. Jennifer dreamed, but it was I who had to draw the dreams from her and steady them. Rosalind was Clara's favourite, but she had jibbed at learning what she most wanted to know. And didn't the ghosts themselves appear only to me?

As I sat in a corner of the college canteen, scowling like someone agonizing over a crossword clue, and feeling as lonely as a monolith on a moor, Jennifer came up and took the chair opposite me.

'I've got a theory,' she said.

'How nice.'

'I don't think Alice and Clara were enemies.'

She'd hinted at this before. 'So how do you explain Clara brandishing a knife over Alice's body?'

'Mustn't jump to conclusions.'

'Jen, if you've come along just to be clever–'

'Listen, will you. Alice kept at me for days and days and made me ill, and I don't know what she wanted to tell me, but there was no hate in it. I've got the feel of her and I know it. She wanted to put things straight and couldn't. Don't ask me what she wanted to put straight. Whatever it was she's never been able to say. But they didn't hate each other, not really. That was a myth made up by their mother and believed in by people like Mrs Porter.'

'Weird thing to make up.'

'Jealousy. No-one else must love Alice. But people behave as they're expected to. Especially children. Yes, I know, I've said that before. They lived up to it and actually believed it themselves in a way, but it wasn't true.'

'Rosalind would be glad to hear this.'

'Clara's girl. Yes. I think I've misjudged Clara.'

'Are you changing sides?'

'No, still pro-Alice.'

'So what's to do?'

'Rosalind and I should stop feuding and team up.'

'Now you're talking! Haven't I always said–'

'Ah, but this is it. Sounds easy. Like, make alcoholics give up booze and they'll be all right. Rosalind will agree, we'll all agree, we'll sign a contract if you like, but we've to *feel* it. Here.' Jennifer jabbed her slight bosom with her forefinger. 'Not easy, John.'

'It's a start,' I said. And immediately I felt more alone than ever.

My father was right, Jennifer was ultra-sensitive. Perhaps that was why she had a sharp tongue: self-protection. The rose and thorn. I thought that rather neat, but I would never have dared say it to her. She'd have fallen about. A pity, though. Why must we so often hide our feelings?

That had been the trouble with Alice and Clara, hadn't it? Jennifer thought so.

But where did we go from here? Team up? How do you make people 'love each other'? I thought of various crazy situations where one girl did the other some overwhelming service.

'I hate people who do me good turns,' said Jennifer.

I wondered if she would make any overtures to Rosalind, but of course she was too intelligent for that. Neither did I say anything to Rosalind myself. Useless. I knew what she'd say. 'Of course I'd like to cooperate with Jennifer. No, I do not dislike her . . .' And she'd remain unconverted.

In any case, even if the girls had their arms round each other's necks, what help would that be? How did we know that Alice and Clara weren't doomed to go on with their fruitless haunting for the rest of time? What did we really know about them? Mere scraps. Perhaps this was a family curse like the legendary ones you read about, and not meant to end.

We went dancing again that evening, which was at least a good way of avoiding conversation that lately was becoming morbid. I had foolishly suggested the idea of a 'family curse' to Rosalind, and she had immediately related it to herself. That experience at the Rainham had knocked the stuffing out of her, and she was beginning to have awful misgivings, not only about Clara, but herself as well. Perhaps she wasn't worthy of

111

the perfect family she had always dreamed about. Perhaps she was doomed to pay for the sins of her parents. It all sounded far-fetched and ridiculous, but once you let a fear get hold of you, it will eat your heart out. Underneath the handclapping and hipswitching she did so well, she was subdued and rather shamefaced, and although for once I was very patient I could not talk her out of it.

I saw her home and walked back, very depressed. The curse idea was catching. Why should I suffer everyone else's hang-ups? Had Clara intended it, even? Was that why she had left my parents the shop, that too easy windfall—so that I should pay for it? I turned dejectedly into the high street.

I was tired, not so much from the long walk as from all the mental exercise during it. I plodded down the high street on the opposite side from our shop and then without bothering to look round, strode out into the road. There was a screech of brakes and a scurry of tyres. I looked behind me in a kind of frozen calm. The car moved on: none of the hooting and flashing and fist-shaking that are common in these cases. I expected the driver to stop and come grimly up to me, but he did not, and I was alone in the high street, unhurt and curiously unshaken.

Cars interest me. The receding back of this one did so exceedingly. It was a vintage car in beautiful condition, a Hispano Suiza, round about 1920, worth a fortune.

I had better get out of the middle of the road, though. I crossed to our side of the street and there I saw something very strange indeed. In place of the lamp standard which hung like a petrified brontosaurus over the street at this point, there was an ancient lamppost, with a gas mantle burning in it. I looked up the high street and saw that similar lampposts were positioned up it at intervals, giving out a sickly yellow light that bathed it in a jaundiced haze. And as far as I could tell, the street itself looked different—the shops, the very surface of the road. The dress-shop opposite our own was not there. Very cautiously this time, I crossed the street again and peered up at the building that had taken its place. I made out the name: 'F. Gosling, Family Grocer'.

Some years before, a film company had used our high street for a film about Edwardian England, and had faked the street lights just like this, and had put up false fronts on the shops. Not so extensively as this, though, only at the bottom end of it. Had the same thing happened again? What, in an hour or two? And at night? There seemed no other explanation. They must have flung it up like lightning.

Two men ambled towards me, as if coming from the village pub. They looked like what used to be called 'working men', wearing cloth caps and 'chokers'. Ah, period costume. They were actors. They must be.

'Excuse me,' I said.

They took no notice.

Very uneasy now, I recrossed and went up to our shop. There was no shop. There was a house, bay-windowed, with venetian blinds. There was a front door in a mock-Georgian porch, and a number on the fanlight. 105.

I did not try the front door, but went down the alley on the left and found, sure enough, the side door which we used as our own front door. Would the lock still be the same? Yes, I opened it. Did I in fact open it with my key, or did I just find myself inside?

I went into the front room—the front room, not the shop! This I had seen before. I had seen it in Jennifer's dream. But now I was not dreaming, nor was there any trace of the current. Everything was perfectly solid and everyday: the horsehair sofa, the old armchair with the antimacassar, the more recent stuff—a mix up of pre-1914 and Twenties things. I knew just about enough of antiques to be able to put dates to them.

The only unreal, non-solid creature in the whole scene was myself. I was invisible and inaudible. I was a ghost. Was I dead? That was absurd. Why should I suddenly be dead? And if I was dead, why should I have got into a world of some fifty years before I was born?

I began to roam about the house—or I suppose I did; 'roaming' suggests putting one foot in front of the other, whereas I had only to wish myself somewhere to be there. I roamed in this weightless way up the stairs and past the dolls in their glass cases and into my own bedroom. It was, incidentally, pitch dark, but that didn't seem to matter. In the bedroom a nightlight was burning—a wide, flat candle floating in something in a saucer. It stood on a cabinet beside an iron bedstead. It shone on a girl's head on the pillow. Her face was half-hidden by the sheet, but I knew who it was. Alice, like Jennifer, slept with a light on.

CHAPTER FOURTEEN

Daylight glimmered through the drawn curtains. The night had passed instantaneously; impossible to believe I'd slept through it. On this plane I could move through space and time in flashes, as if in a film.

This was 'my' bedroom. I went and stood beside the fireplace, where I had first seen Alice, and looked round. I saw wallpaper showing arches of roses, and a door painted cream gone cheese-colour, with its panels picked out in wishy-washy blue. The ceiling looked like crazy-paving. A shabby room, but well-furnished. That brass bedstead was worth hundreds, or would be one day. There was a marble-topped washstand which I'd already seen in the basement, a fine mahogany wardrobe, and a gleaming dressing-table laden with little jars and pink-backed hand mirrors and brushes. A fur-trimmed dressing gown was thrown over a chair. Alice's room.

It was cold. I sensed it rather than felt it. I peered through the curtains and saw a milkman's horse in the street below, its nostrils snorting white plumes. The milkman was serving F. Gosling opposite, ladling milk from a churn into a jug. He wore a peaked cap and several layers of waistcoats under his apron.

The pink and cream eiderdown stirred and Alice sat up in bed. I had seen her gaunt and dying, I had seen her in death, but this was more like the Alice I had seen first of all, still cute, though a bit pale and crumpled from sleep. She looked blank and unseeing for a few seconds. Then she seemed to recall something. She gave a moan, covered her face with her hands, and leaned her head on her knees.

The cheese-coloured door opened and the woman I had seen in Jennifer's dream came in. She was fully dressed this time, with her hair 'up' and fastened with combs. She was very like Alice in face. She stood by the bed and put on a weepy look.

Alice lifted her head.

'Do you want something?'

Her mother put her arm round her. 'My poor darling–'

Alice twisted away as though she had been touched with a hot iron.

'My darling, you know there's nothing in this world I wouldn't–'

'You can't do anything.'

'I shan't give up. I shall get more advice–'

'To hear the same thing.'

'Of one thing you may be sure,' said her mother, as if offering the profoundest consolation, 'if my love for you could only–'

Alice twitched again. 'No, don't. Leave me alone. I don't want you, Mother. Leave me alone!'

Her mother looked quite horrible for a moment; then an expression of infinite forgiveness took over her face.

'Very well, my darling. Mary shall bring in your breakfast.'

She went out slowly, wronged, dignified and noble, but Alice didn't consider her; she was staring in my direction, round-eyed and frightened, for something had happened between us. 'I don't want you'–that was a speech I had heard before. Recognizing it, I gasped, or did whatever my disembodied state allowed. And Alice heard me, or felt the effect, somehow, and her room became haunted.

The maid, Mary, came in, bringing tea and waferish bread and butter and a boiled egg. This was Rosalind's Mrs Porter, in her twenties, wearing a frilly cap and a white apron over a skirt which reached almost to her ankles. She was plump and rosy, with dark hair curtaining her cheeks. She put the tray beside the bed and gave an authentic little Upstairs-Downstairs bob. I waited for her to say 'Beggin' your pardon, Miss,' but what she did say was, 'Here you are then, Miss Alice. Eat it up, now.'

'Like a good girl,' said Alice.

'It's a nice egg,' said Mary apologetically, and stood irresolute, her head slightly tilted.

'Will you do something for me, Mary?'

'Of course, Miss.'

'Then stop looking at me like a dying duck, or I shall scream.'

Mary looked hurt, and Alice began to apologize; but then she was struck again with the same shock she had received from my ghost of a gasp. Once again I recognized what she said: 'like a dying duck . . . I shall scream'–I had heard it before; or I suppose, by chronological reckoning, I was going to hear it again. I gave a bound of recognition. Alice stopped in mid-speech; she caught her breath; she gasped. Mary leaned over her in alarm.

'Oh, what is it? Is it the pain again?'

'No . . . no. It's just . . .' She looked up, blanched and terrified, a chic nineteen-twenties flapper suddenly aware of mortality. She laughed a very wan laugh. 'I think someone's walking over my grave, Mary.'

'That's just a saying, Miss–'

'Mary, I'm going to die.'

'You mustn't talk like that.'

'But I am. You know I am.'

'You mustn't say so. You mustn't give up hope.'

'I've got T.B. and I'm going to die. I'm sorry I was rude. Please go away.'

Mary edged out with apprehensive backward glances, and I watched Alice spooning her egg. She was so like Jennifer. Not so much facially–although you could recognize the family lines–but in her being–her air, her speech. I connected with her. There was a current between us.

Now Clara came in, wearing gloves and a long overcoat with a fur collar. She had fine eyes and a well-cut face. You could see that she was Alice's sister, but she was another kind of person.

'I'm going shopping. Anything I can get you?'

'Would you get me a "Lady's Companion"?'

'Righto. Anything else?'

'No . . . Clare?'

'M'm?'

'Do you believe in premonitions of death?'

'Oh dear oh dear,' said Clara, and sat down on the bed. She pushed Alice's fringe back from her forehead and gave her a small, dry smile. 'No, I don't think so. Probably hokum! Like Old Moore's Almanac!'

'Just imagination?'

'I think you could bet on it.'

'You've cheered me up!'

'Tell you what, I'll cheer you up even more and bring back some cigarettes.'

'Oh, would you? Don't let Mother know.'

'You'll have to smoke them up the chimney. The exercise will do you good.'

'Thanks, Clara. Thanks.'

For a while after Clara had gone, Alice looked almost happy. But gradually her face lengthened and at last she began to cry, quietly and unrestrainedly, the tears welling up and rolling down her cheeks. I felt so sorry for her that I did something very wrong. I went to her and gently took her hands. As soon as I did so she stared wildly, her mouth opened, she went whiter than ever and she fell back, a long hoarse rattle coming from her throat. This, too, I had heard once before.

The breakfast tray slipped to the floor and the teapot capsized. Alice lay white and still. I began ranging the house, convinced that I had killed her, desperate to arouse attention and hopelessly unable to do so.

Time began again to move in jerks. I was back in Alice's room with Clara, her mother, and the doctor. The mother sat huddled in a corner, weeping and twisting her fingers. Clara maintained an icy self-control, speaking curtly and frowning as if she were angry. The doctor listened to his stethoscope.

'She is alive.'

After a time he added: 'I cannot quite understand this. Her condition has not worsened and she has not had a stroke. She's in a deep faint, as far as I can tell. As if she'd had a bad shock. Has she had a shock?'

'You were the last person with her,' said her mother to Clara, in a tragically accusing way.

'She was all right when I left her.'

'She was not *all right,* she was very ill.'

'Yes yes Mother. You know what I mean.'

'There! Can't you hear the impatience in your voice? The evil temper? Don't you think *that* could shock her, delicate as she is?'

'Mother,' said Clara, with grim patience, 'I did not give her any sort of shock.'

'I should have known better than to leave her to your tender mercies.'

The doctor coughed. 'She's coming round. Don't let her hear any discord.'

'No, I should think not,' said the mother indignantly.

Alice's eyelids fluttered. After a while she began to ask questions, directing them at Clara over the head of her palpitating mother, who was now all but lying on top of her.

'I wasn't here,' said Clara. 'It seems you fainted. Don't worry.'

'Don't *worry!*' moaned the mother. 'Oh no, she mustn't *worry!*'

She stayed by the bedside for a good two hours after this, keeping vigil as Alice slept, or rather, tried to sleep, for her mother kept tenderly waking her to assure her that there was nothing she wouldn't do for her. Able to by-pass time as I was, I saw this period through quite quickly. At last Alice sat up and said, 'I want to see Clare.'

'Oh no, darling, that wouldn't be wise—'

'I want to see her!'

'Just for a few minutes, then,' said her mother, pursing her lips.

The sisters spoke in whispers, with good sense, for I could confirm their suspicion that their mother was listening behind the door.

'She hovers over me like a vulture,' said Alice.

'She cares for you.'

'Cares for herself.'

'Don't be too hard on her.'

'You're too soft on her. You're a mug . . . Clare (keep our voices down)—you thought I was dead, didn't you?'

'You gave us a fright, yes, but—'

'No buts. You did. The doctor did at first. *I* did. Clare, I felt Death touch me!'

Clara paled, and gave her sister that stern searching look that was her own strange way of showing concern, but she replied quite lightly, 'Well! but here you are, still around!'

'But that's it. You all thought I was dead. It could happen again. Worse. It could last for days. Clare, they could bury me alive!'

'Oh, shut up, will you? Do you think I'd let them?'

'You mightn't know. Clare! Promise me! When it happens—'

'Shut up, now,' said Clara, trembling.

'Promise me, Clare. Make sure that I am dead!'

Hearing this again struck me with the fiercest pang of all. The shock of my recognition hit the sisters too, and for a moment I saw them cling to each other in mortal terror.

But the scene scrambled before my eyes. My senses reeled and swooned, and when the scene formed again I was in the hideous basement as the knife fell from Clara's hand, and her mother staggered across the room to collapse at her feet. I was as bewildered and confused as they, but one thing was certain for me now: Clara was not evil; Rosalind had been right about her, she was good, she was good, however black it looked, and I wanted to tell everyone, Clara, the poor body of Alice, Mary the maid who now stood trembling with fear at the foot of the steps, and the gibbering hulk of the mother herself–I would tell them, they must listen . . .

But this scene was more than I could bear, and once again I couldn't hold it in focus. It swung about me, it broke up, it went round and round before my eyes. Round and round . . . until it seemed that I could even hear a voice saying 'round, round'; and then I saw a watch pinned to the chest of a white uniform, and the voice said:

'He's coming round, Sister.'

I raised my eyes from the watch and took in the neat nurse herself.

'What–?'

'Easy,' said the Sister, from the other side of the bed.

'A car knocked you over in the high street,' said the nurse placidly.

'A Hispano Suiza?'

'I wouldn't know!'

I struggled to sit up. 'I must see Rosalind and Jennifer–'

'Easy,' said the Sister, pressing me back. 'You shall see them in good time.'

The nurse stuck a thermometer in my mouth.

CHAPTER FIFTEEN

My left wrist was in plaster and I had mild concussion. I had been very lucky. I had stepped right out into the road without warning. If the driver hadn't reacted so promptly, etc, etc . . .

Hispano Suiza?

No! Peugeot . . .

I lay back in the disillusionment of daylight. If you don't pull yourself together, I told myself, you'll end up in a nut-house.

It had been a dream, just a lousy dream. What a let-down! What a sickening let-down!

How long have you been kidding yourself, John Crawley, dud twin fit only to do fix-it jobs?

I lay back in the white bed in the white ward where everything, even to the voices of the nurses, might have been swabbed with disinfectant and made it the unspookiest place on earth, and felt sick with self-disgust. In this state, awash with disenchantment and commonsense, I tried to act as my own psychiatrist.

Well, of course, I and I alone had been the one to *see* anything. And I only saw things – this was true every time – after the idea of them had already been put in my head. Like an anthropologist who constructs a whole prehistoric man from a fragment of bone, I built up a family history out of hallucinations and a few scraps of evidence.

But why should I?

Well, the psychiatrist would go back to my childhood, and

Jennifer's spooky tales. He would say I still believed them, in a form more suited to my age. Look how I'd carried on the image of the full moon–didn't Jennifer first put that into my head?

What about Jennifer?

Well, the current was real enough. We interacted. Jennifer discovered that she knew just how Alice felt, and I discovered that Jennifer looked just like Alice! She influenced me, I influenced her, and she brought forth an Alice just like herself.

Rosalind?

Rosalind had the orphan's dream of a family: she adopted Clara and idealized her. I wanted Clara to be good for Rosalind's sake, but at the same time I was jealous of Rosalind's love for Clara, and so I compromised, and invented a Clara who seemed hard as nails and yet was a good sort underneath . . .

How to explain all the things that had happened to the girls, then?

If you doubted the power of suggestion, just remember that a whole Home full of girls got hysterics from it . . .

Basically, the psychiatrist would say, now full steam ahead and bursting with confidence, basically, it all hung on jealousy–jealousy and guilt. I was jealous of Jennifer, Daddy's little wonder, she was jealous of Rosalind, and Rosalind was jealous of her, the clever, possessive twin sister. And we all felt guilty for feeling jealous. And between us we made up our own myth.

So far from the girls 'drawing strength from me', I'd surely conned them into having delusions.

And it had got to stop.

A nurse came up, bringing me a drink on a tray, and I wriggled upright and thanked her politely, just to show how sane and reasonable I was.

Then I lay back again, drained and wan and very sober indeed. I had faced up to the full moon and found it a bubble, and it had burst.

123

It was all perfectly logical. Yet in my heart of hearts I didn't believe it.

Never, the nurses agreed, had they seen such a devoted sister. They could tell that Jennifer was suffering with me every minute. My father proudly told them about our 'telepathy'. Jennifer had the original mind, he explained, and mine was a sort of agent for it. Fancy, they said. I don't think they understood him.

And such a doting girl-friend too!

'Lucky chap,' said the young doctor who signed my discharge. 'Surrounded by adoring girls!'

But I wasn't grateful. I wondered what freak fantasies had been possessing them while I was on my hallucinatory trip to 1923. I felt severe, like a Victorian father. They must be brought to their senses.

Hospitals discharge you quickly these days, and I was out the next afternoon; but I still felt shaky, and my mother consigned me to bed. That evening, making it respectable by being together, the girls visited me in my room.

As soon as I saw them, I realized that something amazing had happened. They were friends. God knows how or when this bit of chemistry took place. It must have worked on them unawares, like measles. I had always longed for it. But you are not always pleased when you get what you want, and now I felt uneasy, as if they were in league against me.

They settled down, Rosalind on the end of my bed and Jennifer in the armchair.

'Tell us, then,' said Jennifer.

'Tell you what?'

'Come on, stop stalling.'

'Is it bad?' asked Rosalind anxiously. 'Is it painful to tell? Because we can stand it, you know—'

'There's nothing.'

'What do you mean, nothing?' demanded Jennifer.

'I tell you, there's nothing.'

'Look, John, from the time they scraped you off the high street till you came round, I was getting the hell of a buzz that nearly knocked my head off, and don't tell me you don't know because I know perfectly well you do. Why, Dad's been bragging to the entire hospital about it! "John interprets for Jennifer!" Go on, then, interpret, brother.'

'And I got these dreams,' said Rosalind. 'All night long. Voices. But it was like they were talking in some foreign language. Couldn't make out a blind word. But terrifically uptight.'

'Well, only dreams,' I said.

'Why only?' said Jennifer.

'Well, dreams aren't real.'

'Has some shrink in the hospital been getting at you?'

'No, I've been my own shrink.' And I told them how I'd worked it all out, and rejected the supernatural and burst the bubble.

'*Now* he tells us,' said Jennifer.

'It's high time,' I said.

'Well, well,' said Jennifer. 'What silly deluded girls we've both been, for sure. And how lucky to have such a level-headed male to put us right! And now everything's in order, is it?'

'Go easy,' said Rosalind anxiously. 'He's not well.'

'This won't break his arm in any more places,' said Jennifer callously. 'Listen, John. All my life I've been frightened of the dark, and I've always dreaded people finding out, I'm so ashamed of it. But it's not my fault, and I know why now. I'm haunted. I always have been haunted. And I shall go on being haunted till this is cleared up.'

'I am trying to clear it up,' I said. 'I'm looking at it reasonably.'

'Psychiatry for Everyman,' said Jennifer. 'In paperback, three ninety-five. You're not clearing it up, you're ruining it. It isn't a thing you can reason about, it's not a head thing, it's a blood thing, in the blood –'

'Yes,' said Rosalind, nodding, 'that's what it is. I loved Clara and she loved me and she's been trying to get through to me, and you just can't reason that away, because it's still there when you've finished.'

'You just *want* to believe it all, don't you?' I demanded.

'Yes,' said Rosalind simply.

'Well, you must count me out.'

'That's just it,' said Jennifer grimly. 'We can't. For some God-known reason, we have to rely on you.'

I felt far, far less sure of myself now, but I hung on.

'I'm not going to kid myself any longer, Jen.'

'You've *started* kidding yourself, that's what,' said Jennifer. 'You ought to make sand boxes for ostriches.'

At last they left me, agreeing, no doubt, that men were deceivers ever. I felt guiltier than ever. What you sow, you reap. I had put the idea of haunting into their heads, and now I couldn't make them lose it.

There was a tap at the door and my mother came in.

'Not feeling too good?'

'I'm all right.'

'I thought the girls seemed rather concerned.'

'How was Rosalind?'

'Rather miserable. Laughing much too much at Dad's jokes.'

'I wish he didn't have to make those ghastly jokes.'

My mother smiled her tired, patient smile and sat at the head of the bed, next to me.

'Don't be too hard on him. He's really very proud of you.'

'Har, har.'

'But he is. And though I shouldn't say it, just a bit jealous, too.'

'What the hell's he got to be jealous about?'

'Well, your powers.'

'Oh, yes, he's got some thing about Jennifer and me. I don't rate that.'

'Well, you ought to. He said–now let me see, what did he say?–He said, "I admit that I've been blind to the fact that John has rare psychological acumen".'

'He means that I'm a stooge for Jennifer.'

'If you take it like that you're simply running yourself down. It does him credit, because he does like to think he's the voice of authority, and it's been very hard for him to face up to it.'

'Face up to what? Do *you* think I've got this rare psychological thingummy?'

'I don't put things the way your father does, but . . . Well, I do think that you worry tremendously about other people's feelings. I was worried at first when that child so went overboard for you, but I must say you've treated her very sympathetically.'

'How, Mum?'

'You understand her needs. Her touching interest in Aunt Clara's album, for instance–you've been very sweet and patient about that. You can't be all that interested in Dad's family tree.'

Which proved that she had no idea of what had really been worrying us. But she saw into us for all that.

'It may be,' said my mother, 'that you don't think quite enough of yourself.'

I certainly thought a lot *about* myself, but she had given me a whole new outlook. Worried about other people? Yes, I was.

Jennifer had once said that people act as they're expected to. Yes, till someone suggests a different act . . . And although I had sworn to banish them from my mind, I couldn't help thinking of Alice and Clara, or our own versions of them, if you like–and the roles they had been expected to play . . . They'd needed someone to show themselves to themselves differently, someone like my mother . . . whose blood was in my veins . . .

No! I told myself firmly. Don't go back on that track. I had peopled the full moon with the wrong characters. Alice and Clara had been merely symbols.

All the same, my mother had stirred up a swarm of reflections, and for most of the night I could not sleep.

CHAPTER SIXTEEN

A day or two later I went back to college, and my friends wrote their signatures on my plaster. I can't clearly remember what I did for the next few days. It's as if I slept through them. As I couldn't drive the car, or go dancing, Rosalind would call round in the evenings, and the family would let us be alone together in the kitchen. Trying to cuddle someone on an upright chair when you can only use one arm is not very satisfactory.

Rosalind was behaving like a patient wife who has taken her husband for better, for worse and is enduring a stretch of worse. She agreed meekly with everything I said. She seemed at the same time to be watching for chances of reopening The Subject, but she said nothing, and I couldn't find fault with her. Jennifer was keeping quiet, too. If she was having any dreams, she was keeping them to herself. I felt quite sad about this, as if I were mourning a loss. I really was very fond of Jennifer. I didn't want a stranger in her place.

Nothing might ever have happened. No ghost returned. The basement and its dolls, the shop with its couch, my bedroom, were as unevocative as an empty grate. It was like a finished love affair, when you look back at that other person who was yourself in love, and can't recall his feelings.

The girls were very friendly now, not with the old artificial mateyness, but with real closeness, and I was sure they discussed Alice and Clara behind my back. It made me feel out of it, like some old crab of a father whose children have a conspiracy against him, and I felt some sympathy for my own father, and his wish to be liked.

Several weeks went by. My arm came out of plaster. Life was rather hollow. I've never been a smoker, but people who have given up smoking have told me that it could feel like this.

On the Friday before half-term, at the time of year when there were slippery wet leaves in the streets, my parents went to the theatre with some friends. The three of us went to the pictures. I sat between the girls and held Rosalind's hand while Jennifer stared fixedly at the screen throughout; but I had a weird feeling that Rosalind, metaphorically speaking, was holding hands more with Jennifer than with me.

This feeling grew stronger as we made our way home. We all three were chatting together quite normally, but there was a sense of strangeness about both of them, and I was at a loss to define it.

My parents were going on to a dinner after the show, and would be home very late, and my mother had left a cold supper for us in the back room. There were two chairs on one side of the table, and one on the other, facing the shop. I went to take the chair next to Rosalind.

'Sit opposite us, John,' she said, 'so we can both look at you.'

Now this had the sort of innocent cunning about it that she sometimes used when she was contriving to get us alone together, and although I took the other chair meekly enough, I was sure by now that they were working out some plot between them. Jennifer began slicing up the pork and chicken pie and I sawed up some malty loaf and buttered it, and we all three talked of the film and this and that, and nothing could have sounded more ordinary; but it was all false, it was like those phoney chit-chats the girls used to have, it hid something else. I began to suspect that they were literally not themselves: they were being used.

My determination to clear my head of superstition was weakening like a New Year Resolution in mid-January. There was a presence in the room with us, so strong that it made all previous contacts seem like tricklings through a dam. The girls chatted on, but I was staring between them into the shop, and they went out of focus and almost out of sight. All that wise thinking about imagination was forgotten now. This was no more imaginary than toothache is. So strong was it that I expected the whole scene to go back in time, the lighting turning to gas and the shop to a front room; but nothing changed, only the presence grew so urgent that it was like physical pressure, as if the walls were closing in.

I had a faint, sidelong vision of the girls now, as if they were mere outlines. They have turned to ghosts, I told myself. By shifting my eyes I could have made them solid again, but my gaze was fixed and my eyes began to blur and dazzle, and in the halo of light caused by this I began to see sights.

They would not hold steady: a succession of jumbled images. The details of the room had dissolved in the light, and in the centre I saw flashes and glimpses of the family past. I saw a tiny girl in a ballet skirt, curtseying. I saw an older child, hurt and rueful, clutching a doll and setting her face against tears. I saw Alice enduring some compulsory fondling on her mother's lap. I saw Clara raging with temper. I saw Alice in costume after costume. I saw Clara looking on.

The visions died away. The region of the shop grew dark. For a brief moment I saw Alice and Clara clear and solid: Alice the chic flapper as I had seen her first of all, and Clara the gaunt old lady of eighty-five. They loomed out of the darkness and drifted towards our table. They vanished in the light.

And now I saw Rosalind and Jennifer again plainly. They were staring at me. The eyes they were staring with were not their own.

It is more frightening than any ghost to see the eyes of people you love estranged like this. I was looking at Rosalind and Jennifer, but the eyes of Clara and Alice stared back at me through the masks of their faces. But the shock died away as I stared back. When you think of people being 'possessed', you naturally think of evil, of devils. This was nothing of the kind. The strange eyes pleaded with me and implored me, and I realized with wonder that they needed me.

They had got this far because Rosalind and Jennifer were now in harmony; but they could get no further without me. They had needed the girls only to reach me. Indeed, they needed all three of us together. Hence all the hassle they had previously caused the girls. Hence the futile mouthings when they had confronted me before.

So I was the final aid. I had known this all along in a vague sort of way, but all the same it amazed me. I, John Crawley, the family fix-it man: I mattered this much. It seemed that my father, of all people, had been right. Maybe I did have this 'psychological acumen',–which, when translated, I took to mean simply understanding people better than average. Did I? I had been wrong most of the way, and I had been wrong most of all about myself.

The sisters, their eyes still fixed on me, began speaking through the mouths of the girls.

You might expect ghosts to speak high-flown and solemn, like old-time Shakespearean actresses. But when Alice spoke through the mouth of Jennifer she sounded brittle and tetchy, like Jennifer herself.

She said: 'What went wrong?'

From the mouth of Rosalind the aged rasp of Clara's voice replied: 'I kept my word. I meant to do it.'

I did not understand this, but there was no way I could interrupt. Alice's voice said: 'It would have made no difference. I was dead already. What stopped you?'

'Mother.'

'She found you at it?'

'There was a terrible scene.'

'Yes,' said the voice of Alice bitterly, 'she came between us all our lives, and she's between us still.'

132

I wanted desperately to speak to them. I wanted to say, 'Alice, your sister loves you. She has always loved you. Your mother has kept you apart only because you have let her. She has power over you only because you think she has. No-one can stop two people loving each other if they have a mind to it. There's no barrier. Give in. Join each other.'

But my mouth was dry. Who was I, seventeen years old, to preach sermons to these two? Even in normal circumstances I had always found it hard to express my feelings. I could tell Rosalind I loved her, in a sexy way, but with everyone else I was tongue-tied. I loved Jennifer, but to say so would have choked me. This was worse. I was speechless.

Instead, I reached out, trembling and tentative, and took each girl by the hand.

As I did so I remembered the awful effect this had had on Alice in my dream. I might, I thought, cause some fearful spiritual short-circuit.

But for once I had done the right thing. The sisters needed just this link, this contact. Words are ambiguous and treacherous. This was the feeling itself. The current ran through my arms and flared in my head. For an instant I felt such a charge of love that not all the songs in the world together could contain.

And then a sort of clearing of my head. Something like the cracking of your ears when you recover from a deaf spell. Or breaking surface after a dive. Or spotting the answer to a sum. I'm sorry I can't put it more elegantly. The coin dropping.

Full moon.

I had never worked this image out properly. I had seen Alice as one crescent and Clara as the other. You can't complete a circle with two crescents or quarters. You need a middle bit. I had found the middle bit. Myself. Why it had to be me I can't explain, except perhaps that I was young, and in love.

Jennifer was saying something quite trivial, like 'Another bit of pie?' and Rosalind was saying, 'Oh, no thanks,' and it seemed that time must have been suspended while all that was going on, and they had no inkling of it. And then, without a pause or any change of manner, they looked at each other, and Rosalind said:

'You know what Clara meant to do?'

Jennifer said, 'Yes. Cut her wrists.'

'That's right. Cut her wrists.'

They had inside knowledge from literally inside sources, and I still could not see the point of what Clara meant to do; but there was no time to go into details. They both looked at me, and Jennifer spoke with more affection than I should have thought possible from her.

'John? All right now?'

'Yes, it's all right now.'

Their faces cleared as if they had both awakened with great relief from a dream, and Rosalind said:

'They've gone, haven't they?'

I nodded, and Rosalind nodded too, with absolute conviction, as if she had received divine proof.

'Yes,' she said, 'they've gone.'

'For good,' I said.

The girls explained later what that 'cutting of the wrists' was all about. Alice, as I knew already, had a dread of being buried alive. If her wrists were cut, and no blood came, it would prove that she was really dead. And this she must have persuaded Clara to do.

So Clara tried to keep to her gruesome promise. If she looked hard-eyed and haggish, like a murderess, no wonder. Her whole being must have revolted against it. She stood on the very brink of the act. Her mother was shocked into madness. She died believing that her monstrous daughter had been going to mutilate the body.

Clara kept herself going by closing her heart to all softer

feelings. Marriage, a cosy domestic life with Basil, was out. She became a hard business woman with a bitter tongue. She became odd. People were scared of her and suspected her of strange dealings, but in fact she was haunted by a spirit as bewildered as herself, and even after her death she could not communicate with her.

Did I really go back in time, a ghost from the future, to reach people living many years before I was born? Are there other time systems than our own?

The tame psychiatrist inside me would say that I had gone back in imagination, and that what I thought I saw was really inspired guesswork on my part.

But I can't persuade the medium inside me against his will.

And that's about all, except that my mother, not long afterwards, in her weirdly intuitive, vague fashion, said:

'John, promise me something. You'll never go near a spiritualistic séance.'

Promising this was easy. You might as well ask someone who has just been dragged out of a fire not to jump back into the flames.

POSTSCRIPT

'Forgotten already?' I said.

Rosalind raised her head from my shoulder for a moment.

'No, of course not. I can remember everything. All we did, and that. It's just that it doesn't, like, seem real any more.'

'Jennifer's the same. She says that in six months she won't even remember their names.'

Rosalind settled her head again.

'Oh, well, never mind.'

'All the same–'

'Don't go on about it, love.'

'Who's been so uptight about it for so long, then? "It doesn't seem real any more"! So what's real?'

'This is,' said Rosalind.